THE WORM AND THE STAR

John Fuller is an acclaimed poet and novelist, author of thirteen volumes of verse and several works of fiction. *Flying to Nowhere* was shortlisted for the Booker Prize and winner of a Whitbread Award. He is a Fellow of Magdalen College, Oxford.

D1589355

9 39824569

ALSO BY JOHN FULLER

Poetry

Fairground Music
The Tree that Walked
Cannibals and Missionaries
Epistles to Several Persons
The Mountain in the Sea
Lies and Secrets
The Illusionists
Waiting for the Music
The Beautiful Inventions
Selected Poems 1954 to 1982
Partingtime Hall (with James Fenton)
The Grey among the Green
The Mechanical Body
Stones and Fires
Collected Poems
The Vintage Book of Love Poetry (editor)

Fiction

Flying to Nowhere
The Adventures of Speedfall
Tell it me Again
The Burning Boys
Look Twice: An Entertainment
A Skin Diary
Memoirs of Laetitia Horsepole

Criticism

A Reader's Guide to W. H. Auden
The Sonnet
The Dramatic Works of John Gay

For Children

Herod Do Your Worst
Squeaking Crust
The Spider Monkey Uncle King
The Last Bid
The Extraordinary Wood Mill and Other Stories
Come Aboard and Sail Away

John Fuller

THE WORM
AND THE STAR

VINTAGE

Published by Vintage 2001

2 4 6 8 10 9 7 5 3 1

Copyright © John Fuller 1993

The right of John Fuller to be identified as the author of
this work has been asserted by him in accordance with the
Copyright, Designs and Patents Act, 1988

This book is sold subject to the condition that it shall not by
way of trade or otherwise, be lent, resold, hired out, or
otherwise circulated without the publisher's prior consent
in any form of binding or cover other than that in which it
is published and without a similar condition including this
condition being imposed on the subsequent purchaser

First published in Great Britain in 1993 by
Chatto & Windus

Vintage
Random House, 20 Vauxhall Bridge Road

**Bedford
Borough Council**

9 39824569

Askews & Holts

The Random House Group Limited Reg. No. 954009
www.randomhouse.co.uk

A CIP catalogue record for this book
is available from the British Library

ISBN 0 09 942198 4

The Random House Group Limited supports The Forest Stewardship
Council (FSC®), the leading international forest certification organisation.
Our books carrying the FSC label are printed on FSC® certified paper.
FSC is the only forest certification scheme endorsed by the leading
environmental organisations, including Greenpeace. Our
paper procurement policy can be found at
www.randomhouse.co.uk/environment

Printed and bound in Great Britain by Clays Ltd, St Ives PLC

Contents

Contents

The Worm and the Star

I
TRUE OR FALSE

The Memoirs of Achilles

Until Achilles deigns to publish his memoirs we shall really know almost nothing about him.

This may turn out to be the supreme paradox associated with his name. Nothing else will haunt us in quite the same way. How could it be, generations will ask, that you all pretended to be familiar with the exploits of this hero? You were waiting for revelations, for corroborations of rumours, simply, after all, for plain facts. And you had nothing. How shall we reply? That we were content with the legend? That we had no real hope of ever learning anything like the truth?

That would be one defence. And it would be a defence flattering to Achilles, who is in any case exactly the sort of hero who needs flattering the most. Simply to be a hero, then, would be quite enough for him. And for us too, is the implication. Try telling that to Hector's children!

There is another defence. We might say that we never believed any of the stories in the first place. It would be quite easy to claim that Achilles had no unusual qualities after all, that he was essentially no

3

different from you or me. It would be properly democratic to take this line. It isn't an age of heroes.

Why, then, are his memoirs so eagerly awaited? Is it that our favourite reading is the extraordinary luck of the otherwise perfectly ordinary man? Do we simply have a craving for the supernatural? Perhaps. We want him to be beyond human weakness without ever giving up some of the most sordid human emotions: idleness, anger, self-esteem. We are intrigued by the way it was done, dipped in the divine river by one heel like a fish in batter. O the perfect transubstantiation! O the delicious god! But when Achilles gets the sulks we shall always forgive him, because there is always something we overlooked, the unsealed corner that is still fish, the weakness that is going to prove the greatest weakness of all.

That's what we most want to know about. What really went on in the court of Lycomedes? What was the nature of his relationship with Patroclus? Why could he never beat the tortoise?

Few of the stories are inherently improbable. Or at least, it is perhaps only our eagerness to know them which contains the seed of their paradoxical nature. It is we who require demi-gods and yet need them to fail. Their adventures are cast in our own image, our own sense of destiny, of monstrous unfairness, of some tiny vulnerability. Perfection is deeply boring. Mere dogged persistence a trap for the smug.

Take that tortoise. Do we find him an instructive

model? Of course we don't. We aren't interested in the apotheosis of a daily routine of anonymous slog. Simply getting there isn't enough, and never having a chance of getting there is equally unpromising. Too human, perhaps. Future generations may be intrigued by that quality of unassuming persistence, of never looking back, but we know better. We like chances to be thrown away.

When Achilles saw the tortoise in the distance ahead we are told that he was relieved, and then amused. Those sedate little pats of dust on the horizon, almost static, pure plod! We know that Achilles kept going, at least at first, but what happened next? Why did he never catch up? What monstrous failure of the will in sight of victory kept him eternally in second place?

We have to hope that his memoirs will throw some light on this incident.

The U-Factor

When I received the letter from Dr L. Liebschmerz of Frumm and Frumm inviting me to work on their latest chess program, you could say I had reason to be flattered. True, I had been involved with my friend Brian Regan's Quickmate for the Archimedes, which had a very friendly write-up in Kevin O'Connell's article in the September 1992 number of *Chess*, but I had no experience in writing for main-frames. Frumm's Stella IV had won the 11th World Computer Championship, one and a half points ahead of Cray Blitz! I packed my bags for Basel immediately.

I should have guessed. What I had thought was my big chance at last turned out to be more like a cattle market. There were hundreds of us. We were all given name-tags and problems to solve, and put into an antiseptic white hall like candidates or patients. I began to regret it. I knew I shouldn't have told Mrs Dodd that she could let my room.

However, talent will out, as they say. I must have done pretty well, because they eventually put me to

6

work on Stella VI, along with a young American called Dick Miller.

It was weeks before we were allowed to meet Dr Liebschmerz. Imagine my surprise on that occasion, when a young woman in rimless glasses and a blue silk suit came into the room. She looked at each of us quite directly, her lips compressed in a half-smile of appraisal, and shook us firmly by the hand.

She told us about the new chips that Frumm had developed, and about the direction that Stella VI was moving in. For the past ten years, she said, chess programmers had been obsessed by power and speed. Existing programs stood or fell by how many possible moves they could consider, how far ahead and how quickly. This was no good, she had decided. A preliminary necessity, of course, but it led nowhere. Dr Liebschmerz was now working on the U-Factor in computer chess, and we were all put to work on algorithms that would introduce unpredictability into the program.

'Know something?' Dick Miller said to me one day, taking his Staedtler from between his teeth. 'I do believe that Dr Liebschmerz has got the hots for me.'

I was shocked, and tried not to listen to him. I was fairly sure I was near to a break-through in opening response anyway, and kept my head down. I was trying to find a formula that would give the machine an inspirational edge right at the start of the game. Given, say, e4 to respond to, most machines would draw at random on programmed openings and play c5 (the Sicilian) or e6 (the French). Some machines would be set to discover opening theory from scratch, and still probably come up with c5 or e6, or even e5. I wanted to try a third way. Dr Liebschmerz's U-Factor, the element of the unpredictable, the inspirational, the irrational. The intelligent, if you like. The human.

And I solved the problem! Dick Miller was nowhere near. My hard work had paid off, and I'd made my name in the company. A test game was set up, in public, with Sokolov agreeing to be the guinea pig. There were big crowds that night to see him pose for the cameras and crack a nervous joke before making his move: e4.

Stella VI didn't make her move that night, nor the next night. We had to explain to the press the revolutionary significance of the awaited response. Events at the Kursaal for the following week had to be cancelled. The spectators were given passes.

You might have thought from the point of view of the public that it would be considered the biggest flop of all time. Not a bit of it. It was a sensation. The quietly humming Stella was the subject of television jokes. Bookmakers had a field-day, with over 300,000 francs being placed on such unlikely responses as d5 (the Scandinavian). Chess hadn't been so popular all over Europe since the Fischer–Spassky match.

Dr Liebschmerz called me into her office.

'You realise, of course,' she said, taking off her glasses and giving me a slow smile, 'that whatever the outcome, this game is a tremendous success. The value of Frumm shares has risen by over 60 per cent, and the directors of the company will almost certainly give you a very significant advancement.'

I mumbled some demurral. Naturally I was pleased, but as I told her, I needed to see a print-out of Stella's thinking before I could evaluate the significance of my work. If the break-through had indeed materialised, then I was convinced our machine could beat even a world champion.

Dr Liebschmerz came round from behind her desk.

'There are other rewards,' she purred, putting her manicured hand on my shoulder. I froze. Was this to be a condition of my promotion?

Her face approached mine, and I had time to notice the tennis-player's jaw and the tiny lines in her suntan and a faint smell of very good coffee before her lips and tongue entrapped the lobe of my ear and sucked it in like an oyster.

'Did you try this with Dick Miller?' I asked, as coldly as I could.

'Dick wasn't very clever,' she murmured. 'He was too predictable. He tried too hard.'

'I thought we were all supposed to be extremely clever,' I replied. 'Isn't that what the Frumm System is all about?'

9

'I'm not talking about intelligence,' said Dr Lieb-schmerz. 'I'm talking about inspiration.'

Her hands were now working eagerly elsewhere. I pushed her away. I just didn't feel at all inspired in that way. To tell you the truth, I never had.

I was saved for the moment by the buzzer on her desk. A call had come through from the Kursaal. Stella VI had at last, after nearly two weeks, made her own move. Stella VI had resigned.

'I don't understand it,' said Dr Liebschmerz weakly. 'What has gone wrong?'

I couldn't help laughing. My career in Basel was doubly finished. I would have to write to Mrs Dodd to see if her room was free.

'Nothing went wrong at all,' I said. 'It's well known that the second player has an infinitesimal disadvantage and often plays for a draw. The U-Factor turns out to be plain common-sense. Given an insight into human intelligence, Stella has resigned in tribute to it. Really, I'm quite delighted.'

And with that I walked out of the room.

Credulity

The table was in an uproar, so that it was quite a few minutes before the quiet-voiced and mild-mannered Laputin could make himself heard.

'I can tell you what credulity is,' he said, putting a small piece of bread roll into his mouth.

'So could the schoolmaster's wife!' bellowed Ostrolsky, beaming all over his red face as laughter was generally renewed at this coda to his last story. Laputin winced inwardly, and had to wait a moment before beginning again.

'It's a necessary form of self-protection for those of limited understanding,' he said. 'It's also that trust in providence belonging to the absolutely simple life. You must have heard of the Rakusit?'

There were some sniggers from the other end of the table at an inaudible remark from one of Ostrolsky's cronies. It was generally agreed that no one had heard of the Rakusit.

'It is an interesting fact,' said Laputin gravely, adjusting the position of his wine-glass by a millimetre or two with two fingers on its base, on either side of the stem, 'that my grandfather was privileged to see the last surviving member of that nomadic tribe when the man arrived in Moscow in the late 'twenties. It was a sensation. He had made the journey south, some thousand or more miles, on foot.'

The table had fallen silent now. Someone refilled Laputin's glass.

'Yes, almost all we know about that doomed race is due to the one survivor. The Rakusit were optimists. They were optimists in the extreme, their whole way of thinking the very definition of optimism. Let me give you just one example. They lived in the severest of conditions in the far north, but they had no word for *freezing-point*, or, rather, their word for *freezing-point* was *melting-point*. It was the same with their attitude to physical weakness, their description of which was entirely in terms of growing spiritual power. And no wonder. They survived precariously under extreme deprivation. An ancient superstition allowed them to hunt the migrating reindeer only with arrows tipped with reindeer horn. Gradually, over many years, it became clear that they could not kill enough reindeer to maintain a sufficient stock of arrow-heads. Arrows had to be sparingly used. Weak with hunger, the Rakusit hunters took only an uncertain aim. On those rare annual occasions when the tundra thundered with the beat of reindeer hooves, fewer arrows reached their mark.

'The incurable Rakusit optimism turned this ineffectiveness to advantage: the reindeer became a sacred animal, and those members of the tribe who were the earliest to starve became its devotees, assured of immortality as their bodies dwindled. Thus the remaining hunters, fed by tradition on strips of reindeer meat, gradually for that reason became outcasts, haunted by existential guilt.

'The general food became the tundra itself, cut out in rich damp cylinders from the warm plains after the migrations and the failure of the hunt. There was some nutrition in the compressed peat, the network of grass roots, the larvae of beetles, the reindeer droppings and so on, but it was clear that there was not much future for the tribe in what was little more than a diet of earth. And yet that innate Rakusit hopefulness turned earth-eating into a religious belief of profound beauty and simplicity. As vagrant creatures, little more than the racing herds they now failed to catch, they felt divorced from nature. Plugged into the soil, like the unthinking and unrestless plants about them, they experienced a restoration of planetary contact. It was as though, without metaphorical roots, they had managed to acquire real ones.

'Curiously enough, their word for *root* was *nipple*. It seemed to them an identical piece of physiological engineering, the same means of sucking sustenance into the organism. The nipple was very important to the Rakusit, since they were forced to suckle their young well beyond infancy, usually until the age of seven or eight, by which time the male child's physique would tell the parents whether he was destined to be either a guilty hunter, or a dying priest, of the reindeer. Female children would be suckled even longer, almost until the time when, emaciated as they were, they were ready to give suck themselves. For this reason they also called the plugs of earth cut out of the tundra, *nipples*.

'By a very strange coincidence, the existence of the tribe was prolonged for some years by the providential appearance of yet another sort of nipple. Although nothing like *coincidence* appeared in the Rakusit language, since optimists are always expecting something odd to turn up anyway, their notion of providence was perfectly exemplified when an aeroplane carrying a large consignment of tins of Nestlés Condensed Milk crashed near by. The tins were considered miraculous, not only because they combined the shape of the plug of tundra with the substance of the breast, but because they were of such arbitrary and unknown origin. It was perfectly well known to us, however, that Lenin had acquired a taste for condensed milk during his exile in Switzerland, and insisted on its being imported, often secretly and dangerously, even during our own lean years.

'So you see how optimism is the breeding ground of credulity. To the Rakusit, as the lone survivor made clear in his heroic request for fresh supplies, the tins were a divine mutation, a kind of revelation of an

14

evolving diet. As breast to tundra, so tundra to condensed milk, three forms of nipple. It was quite unreasonable, of course. They could just as well have expected to survive on reindeer milk.'

Laputin gave a little cough and looked round the table. His demeanour was so ineffably severe that no one, not even the lewd Ostrolsky, so much as thought of disbelieving him.

The Cretan Liar

I finally ran Epimenides to ground a few miles outside his own village. I caught sight of him from the bus, approaching on his donkey from a side road. 'That's him!' I shouted, and I made the driver stop there and then. I had been pestering all the passengers and riding around all morning from village to village making enquiries. I'd obviously become a source of great amusement, because the passengers let out a cheer when the bus screeched to a halt, and the driver even grinned at me and shook me by the hand.

I waited for Epimenides under an olive tree whose gnarled branches lent some shade to one corner of the burning crossroads. He seemed to take an age to arrive, and from the expression on his face, a combination of irritation, amusement and weary resignation, I could tell that he knew I was waiting for him. But his donkey didn't stop. It went on plodding right past me, its nose in the dust, its old hide creaking like leather. I picked up my knapsack and walked hurriedly beside him, to keep up.

'You've come,' said Epimenides. When I began to

introduce myself he held up one hand. 'I don't want to know who you are. You might be anybody. It doesn't matter to me a bit. Just think how many people might have turned up like this to see me over the last two and a half thousand years! I wouldn't want to know all their names, would I? There wouldn't be any point. That's the price of fame, I suppose, hordes of anonymous admirers.'

I asked him how many there had been.

'None at all, as a matter of fact,' he replied. 'You're the first. But the principle is the same. And interest is bound to grow. Though personally I've never quite seen the point of it all. I mean, almost any Cretan might have said what I said. It was a perfectly unexceptionable thing to say. And yet it was I who said it. I happened to be the one who became well known for saying it. And why was this? Well, you know the answer to that. That's why you're here. I'm well known for saying it because no one can understand it. No one can get their brain around it. It's what I *said* that's become well known. Possibly there are some people who know it extremely well, and indeed are always quoting it to tease their friends, but who tend to forget my name. It's just conceivable that there are a few who have never known my name at all, and think of me as any common-or-garden Cretan. I suppose that is understandable. People in short stories and anecdotes are quite often, for reasons of economy of narrative, presented in anonymity. But you have to remember that they were always, in fact, individuals. Take the seven young men and the seven young virgins we had to sacrifice every year to the Minotaur. They all had names, though you'd never have known it from the legends. When you think how hard it was simply to *find* seven virgins you'll perhaps understand why their families were so disappointed that they were never named. What a matter of pride it would have been! You couldn't compensate for the death of a much-loved daughter, to be sure, but to have her name written down for all time! That's the trouble with legends. They're so unspecific. Any Cretan who made the claim for himself would never be believed. Imagine arriving at the taverna to drink away your grief. You could spend your sacrificed daughter's dowry on wine and cakes for the whole village, night after night, for as long as it might take to convince them, and they'd still never believe you. Because (at the risk of stating the obvious, begging the question and all that) every Cretan is an inveterate liar. And I ought to know, because I'm a Cretan.

'Now listen. If you've come to me for inside information, if you're so obsessed by that little twist in your brain that you've come to have it out with me, to try to discover by staring me in the eyes (*don't* stare me in the eyes like that!) whether what I said was true or false, to bully me into some confession that you'll be privileged to go and trumpet to the rest of the world, then forget it. If this is what fame is really like, being followed by a sweating Englishman in a ridiculous striped shirt, I don't want to know about it.'

And he urged the donkey onwards, away from me, in a dignified but crippled trot.

The Defile

The discovery of eternal life turned out to be the destruction of innocence as well. It may have been the pleasure of seventeenth-century theology to toy with such paradoxes, but for us it was simply the outcome of the natural unwillingness of sentient creatures to have an end put to their consciousness of self. For the only eternal life possible is the life of the mind; matter must decay. The self inheres in the mind. Suppose you could in fact achieve the impossible and preserve a body alive for ever: it would be no good to its owner without the self inhering in it. It would have no consciousness of being alive. But think: the consciousness of being alive is enough for the self. Even the consciousness of being alive in another body.

The interaction of the silicon chip with the brain tissue was a matter of deep controversy in the early 'twenties. However, the ten-volume report presented by Frumm and Frumm to the USE High Court in 2026 was a forensic display of such exhaustive brilliance that there were few legal obstacles after that, only technical ones. The first image to be reproduced on to a computer screen directly from the human thought process was Professor Fussbad's missing lunch (the culminating experiments had gone on for many hours, with much excitement, well into the afternoon and the professor was hungry). From that point it wasn't long before dreams could be stored, and programs for mapping memory developed. By 2039 relatively simple personalities (a week-old child, a catatonic deaf-mute) could be stored on commercial software, and work on re-transference had already advanced considerably. The 'correction' of memory was another High Court issue, and a person's rights to their own experience had to be established on the same sort of basis as artistic copyright. By a simple electronic operation a person could be given a language they had otherwise no time to learn, or (with the appropriate and complicated legal waivers) the remembered sensations of foreign travel or sexual success otherwise denied them by circumstance. This technical expertise was for some years simply a resource for the wealthy, a cross between cosmetic surgery and a library of magical computer games. It was only after complete mental transplants became possible that legislation was passed directing its use (as it should have been in the beginning) into the exclusive sphere of medicine.

We die like soldiers entering a defile. There is no turning back. But the relatively healthy personality rages against this impending separation from the doomed physical body. As death approaches we would be happy to be given another body. Total mind transplants eventually made this possible. Minds could not be stored in machines, but machines could effect the staged interchange of two minds from one body to the other. Physically the process was for the patient as easy as a blood-transfusion, although it took (at least in its early stages) almost two weeks, and cost the equivalent of a four-bedroomed house.

Naturally at first it was not available to all, but the moral problems encountered by the wealthy families who could choose the process in ordinary cases of impending natural death were paradigmatic. Put simply, there was really only a single problem. A self could not yet be stored outside the body. When that day comes the world may largely consist of a vast library of inert, achieved populations in the form of catalogued, even intercommunicating, digitalised minds. But until then a mind, or let us say a 'person', can only be abstracted from its owner's body and put into another body. If a person A is to be 'saved' from death by being put into body B, then person B must either be self-sacrificingly willing to be put into the doomed body A, or must be put into body C. In the second case (which soon became technically possible) the problem is not really resolved, for a home has to be found for person C. And so on.

The first case of simple exchange, often engineered between husband and wife, or between mother and elderly daughter, became known popularly as 'philo-

22

sopher's suicide'. That suicide was involved in the case of volunteer B was not entirely clear, however, for B was not abandoning her own body to oblivion but to the miraculously preserved existence of the beloved A. And A, terminally ill in any case, certainly could not be charged with suicide. But the phrase 'her (or his) own body' was certainly the nub of a philosophical paradox, for in prospect this entity was entirely (and legally) different from what it was at the time of death. At the latter moment B, though shortly to die, had the double satisfaction of seeing her body live and her loved one survive. However, in these simple cases one could not expect this process to continue, however loving and self-sacrificing the members of one's family. The effect would be of one terrified soldier blundering back from the defile, pushing eternally against the stream, forever postponing death for the merest moment.

The second case, where a third body is found, was in every practical sense impossible, even within the most altruistic of families, for the knock-on effect would create chaos in time and expense alone. But a moment's thought gave the answer which an appropriate piece of social legislation soon enshrined as custom. A's personality would not be preserved in B's body, or in C's, but in n's, where n, the unknown, came at the end of the relevant series, at the end of the military file, as the latest of the family. The minds of the dying were, then, exchanged for those of newborn babies, who had absolutely nothing to lose. Who, after all, were fitter to face departure from this life than those who had so recently accomplished the mysterious journey into it? The practice even encouraged the Church to create new rituals and rites of passage, for man now approached death in the state of innocence in which he had been born and might therefore be supposed to be more certainly assured of eternal bliss. To have eternal life of the self on this earth and the eternal life of Beulah at one and the same time! That is a thought indeed.

But as I began by saying, this achieved eternity was effectively for us the end of innocence. Our rosy-cheeked children have the wisdom of sages and they have the hollow eyes of long-suffering. They have minds that can comprehend the infinite and they utter the lewd sniggers of senile roués. Instead of educating our children we are haunted and mocked by them.

Our life is a hell on earth.

The Move

There is always one person who has found you out and makes you feel uncomfortable. However practised your acquired manner or smoothly launched your career, there is bound to be someone who remembers your very first efforts, their ludicrous pretentiousness and your vain attempts to conceal all the rawness beneath them. For me that man was Gideon Black my maths teacher.

I had only to think of his rimless glasses and his smile and the odd backwards angle of his bony face to shudder with self-abasement and irrational hatred. He knew very precisely what my feelings were, and though I had managed to leave school with accolades, perform quite sparkishly at Cambridge and then jump effortlessly on to the information technology bandwagon, it always gave me a terrible sinking feeling to remember his amusement at my grappling with the binomial theorem and to know that he was well aware of the foolish and occasionally quite embarrassing ways in which I had wasted my time at Cornfields.

Perhaps he was jealous of me. I was really doing

quite well, and was singled out for mention when I went back for an old boys' dinner once. Perhaps that was why he bothered to suggest on that occasion that we played chess by correspondence. Perhaps he saw it as a way of preserving his authority, of somehow keeping his eye on me, of making me feel small. He was a demon player who had won his county championship several times in his youth. Over the board he had been merciless with faint-hearted play and had put many small boys off chess for the rest of their lives. I had come near to taxing his abilities in the game, but had never beaten him. To continue to keep me running all over the board at his leisure would be a fine way to keep me in my place. All it needed was that little twice-folded score-card with our addresses already written on it, ready to have some innocuous coded thrust scribbled down such as Qg4 (always a faintly sarcastic move, I thought) and be inserted in a window-envelope and stamped: it was like having his finger and his thumb in a permanently twisted grasp of my ear-lobe. Even the sight of his handwriting made me feel exactly as I did when some awed junior boy would say to me: 'Mr Black's looking for you. Watch out.'

Even after he had inherited the headship at Cornfields and was near to retirement, even after my marriage, when you might have expected me not to care any more, I continued to squirm like a fourth-former when the envelope arrived. Opening it, I would of course find the move I expected to find, the quiet obvious response, the intelligent consolidating move, the cautious exploitative move, the schoolmasterish move. The errors were mine. I never won. He did not need to be brilliant. He played as he had always played, efficiently, without concessions.

My own life took its course, and I can't say that I found much of it very exciting. I was no longer a promising newcomer in my job, my two children seemed disappointingly commonplace and I was bored stiff by my wife's two closest friends. I enjoyed reading, mostly science-fiction, and played a bit of golf. All the time I felt haunted, as though by something important that I'd forgotten to do. Was there some clue to the unremarkable tenor of my life, some critical moment of failure, perhaps a long way back? More and more, particularly when the chess envelope arrived, I would hear the monotonously nasal tones of Gideon Black and see the disgusted expression on his tilted face: 'Pure carelessness, boy. You simply don't take care.'

What might have livened me up would have been to beat him. It might just have given me the confidence to get my act together generally. Silly, when you think of it. Chess is pretty unimportant, and I don't suppose Gideon Black ever thought much about me, except when writing down his irritatingly correct moves in that odd green script of his. But for my part I became more and more obsessed. Even at my now rather advanced age I simply had to prove myself and trounce him just once, to shake off this demon who had me in his grasp.

I knew that it might be done. It was a question of not making mistakes, and of not making mistakes for long enough to induce one's opponent to start making them instead. I really pulled out the stops, but knew, too, that I actually needed a lucky break.

Then it came. I reached the point in a game where, although I was in a sense foolishly overextended, with his queen and a rook marauding strangely and dangerously in my half of the board, I could not only stave off disaster but could, with a sacrifice, obtain a decisive advantage. He believed, I'm sure, that my pair of self-protecting knights were immobilised and therefore no danger. He hadn't seen that by throwing one of them away I could break up his position, and indeed force mate in three. I wrote down the move, inserted the card in the window envelope and posted it with a great lurch of triumph in my solar plexus. This would send my demon howling!

That was on Wednesday. On Friday I opened my paper and read of the sudden death of the Headmaster of Cornfields School, Dorset, Mr Gideon Black, distinguished educationalist etcetera who had in his youth made a remembered contribution to the theory of Fibonacci numbers etcetera unmarried etcetera etcetera. My eye ran down the page expecting some remark about his having been killed by a surprising chess move. I was, I suppose, in a state of slight shock. But then I came to my senses and realised what this meant.

I was foiled of my victory! At the one moment when I had successfully summoned all my powers to defeat him, he simply gave up the ghost without ever even knowing what I had achieved. There was no one else I could boast of it to. I was once more imprisoned in my own mediocrity.

Or was I? On Saturday morning the envelope came back to me. There it was on the doormat, buff like a bill, but pregnant with its consciousness of intellectual effort, almost craven, I imagined, with its admiration of my move and its admission of defeat. He had received the move after all! He died knowing that he was not impregnable. He died knowing at last of what I was capable. This was all that mattered to me. I couldn't feel much grief at his death, but I did feel somehow exonerated. The demon was off my back.

I opened the envelope to gloat over his little green note of resignation. It seemed a suitable colour for the expiry of a demon. I almost laughed aloud.

But he had made no response. All I could see was my own last move, the beautiful sacrifice. There was nothing written in reply. Then I realised what I had done. Careless as ever, even in my triumph, I had folded the card to reveal not his address but my own. I had sent my winning move back to myself, and Gideon Black had died still convinced that I was the fool that I now knew I certainly was.

The Sadness of the Tortoise

You'd think that the tortoise would have become obsessed by the paradox of his victory over Achilles. The lead was insignificant, and yet Achilles never caught up! Imagine him with his cronies in the *Dog and Trumpet*, drinking vodka, peach schnapps and orange-juice (the habitual drink of theatre people) and going over it all, again and again.

'By the time he'd reached my starting point,' he would say, 'I'd moved on ahead, and by the time he'd reached *that* point I'd moved on a bit further. And so on.'

'So he never reached you at all?'

'Not a bit.'

'So the race never finished? You never actually won?'

'I wouldn't put it like that.'

'So why are you here in the *Dog and Trumpet*?'

There'd be no answer to such a line of questioning, so you can understand why the tortoise wasn't eager to invite it. He was quite celebrated enough without encouraging post mortems. As for the awkward fact that there indeed hadn't been anything in the way of a finishing tape, the tortoise suspected that it might help to explain the paradox. Did he actually want it explained? Of course not. That could easily undermine his whole achievement. He could of course make some offhand remark to the effect that the race had never finished *for Achilles*, but it would need a certain deftness of touch. It would have to have been followed by a welcome distraction such as the offer to buy another round of drinks, or some pedant would be sure to raise a voice of rational objection.

No, it wasn't the paradox of his victory which obsessed the tortoise. He had to take the victory for granted or else it might, as you can see, have been somehow taken away from him. He was obsessed by another, fatalistic paradox. If Achilles had failed, against all apparent probability, to catch up with him, was this ludicrous defeat always on the cards? Since what had happened *had* happened, had it been always *going* to happen?

It's a perfectly reasonable obsession. You don't have to explain it by referring to the fact that stage professionals are well known for their addiction to betting on horses. We are all fatalists at some point in our lives, and the tortoise was no exception. It would have made such a difference to his whole life.

'I mean,' he would say, usually towards the boozy end of the evening, 'if I'd *known* that this great success was coming my way, I could have made plans. I would have been a happier person.'

'What would you have done?'

'It isn't so much a question of what I'd have *done*. I just wouldn't have been the tortoise in the sense in which I've been the tortoise all my life.'

'But you couldn't have known.'

'I suppose not, but if I had guessed so, I would have guessed correctly, wouldn't I?'

'The guess wouldn't have been correct until the event itself took place.'

'Why not?'

'Because the future is always inscrutable. Achilles was the fastest runner in the world, and until the occasion on which he failed to catch you up nobody in their right mind would have guessed that a mere tortoise could outwit him. If an outright lunatic had guessed so, no one would have paid him the slightest attention. Hindsight may prove the lunatic correct. So what? It was a mad guess. He didn't *know*.'

The tortoise would look sadly at his nearly empty glass.

'No, but he would have been *right*.'

II

A MATTER FOR SPECULATION

The Courier of Death

On the eleventh of April, quite unannounced and almost unnoticed, the Courier of Death laid his hand on the shoulder of William Hughes of Pentr' er Uchaf.

The village knew about such signs. They were common enough, though feared for their unpredictability and hated for their lack of indiscrimination. Usually they were interpreted as the mark of a chance encounter, an unforced accident with no element of choice, a minor consequence, doubtless, of a grander ambassadorial mission. For Death surely had more important games to play. His armies were already vast, though not, it must be admitted, yet complete. He could hardly be concerned with the details of recruitment. How could his emissaries be given particular persons to seek out? What microscopic vision, what attentive and scrupulous care, was needed to record, to remember and to annotate the names of mere individuals? For his ranks were swollen, weren't they, by the ordinary toll of time? By the known limit of human life? By the very cycle of nature? This seeking out, this unwelcome attention, as by a forgot-

35

ten creditor with his arresting hand, was widely felt to be superfluous. The Courier of Death was agreed to be a creature of whim, playful where his master was stern; arbitrary where his master was just; swift where his master was slow.

But this was a paradox, for in reality the Courier of Death gave the greatest warnings of all. His grasp was so outlandish that it could on occasion be wondered at, boasted of, and even (by the most reckless of villagers, after their third or fourth tankard) claimed as a mark of favour.

To be singled out by Death! To be given such notice! To wonder whose shoulder the Courier's hand had previously rested on, and who was next to be briefly touched, as in the games that the girls and boys played in the school yard, muffled against the cold, chasing and avoiding, shouting with laughter, their cheeks bright as russet pears, their breath living plumes in the frosty air.

'Me next, Ogwen! Catch *me*!'

'Missed me, missed me!'

But William Hughes made no such speculation. He was quite without curiosity as to his placing or precedence in Death's lists. With his eyes tight shut, he lifted up his voice as the midwife held him there, the cord still trailing like a bloody carnival ribbon, and he howled.

On the Rocks

I couldn't help taking notice of the family on the rocks. Anyone would have found it a matter for speculation, the ambiguous relationship between the grave man and the two women, one of whom had to be the mother of the insouciant and independent child of nature. One of them, indeed, but which one? The one who merely sunned herself in indolent and sensual splendour, who might be young enough to be a sister? Or the partly clothed one, more attentive to the child, and who might therefore be employed to be so?

The man showed no greater interest in either. He descended slowly into the water, each forefinger and thumb resting easily on his hips. He wore nothing but a gold pendant, and his gaze was attentive upon the surface of the sea.

What could he see there that so fascinated him? I myself found its creatures cold and strange and never wished them near me when I swam. Whenever it became too hot I would stumble to the edge and flop into the water, and if I happened to open my eyes as I swam out over the deep weeded crevices my sense of the alerted shoals (indistinct in the blur against my stinging eyeballs but suddenly to be noticed in the choreography of flicked tail and massed dash for the deep) gave me an alien shudder.

But this man stared and stared at whatever it was that he could see about his feet, inquisitive, jewelled, fecund. He had no intention of swimming.

The women were soon settled in their clearly habitual attitudes of trance and anointment. The child marched about on the rocks chattering to himself in self-importance. He showed no more interest in the women than his father did. From them there was none of the nourishment, concern, advice or humorous commentary that one might have expected. Their baskets yielded no refreshments. There was no consulting of watches. Nothing but oiled haunches, splayed novels, shut eyelids. Nanny, wife, sister, mother: the roles remained unchosen. This was a family refusing to be a family.

For myself, I was simply amused by these isolated units of narcissism. There was an element of sexual curiosity, even of admiration for the precarious dignity and ostentation of nudity, but no envy or resentment.

Or was there? I considered the possibility that both these women were the man's physical partners. His apparent calm and detachment might simply be the numbed aftermath of erotic indulgence. His mannered patrol of the rocks could signal a public claim to be undaunted by the sexual demands made upon him by

38

the now evidently replete women. His awareness of the attention paid to him by the few other bathers on the rocks, myself included, gave his otherwise motionless posture a slight swivel of arrogance. When his eyes lifted to the horizon it was, it seemed, with the self-satisfied sense of simultaneous weariness and command belonging to a bored sultan.

What then of the child? What afternoon secrets drifted through his busy little head? In what casual performances might he sometimes find himself an innocent participant? What emotions and relationships provided the models for his present solitary games? For he haunted those rocks, and later came back alone from their siesta to continue his quaint play.

It was my fancy that the three were detained at their hotel by some unusual opportunity for excess. The child's high crooning and elaborate collecting of dried reeds seemed to me a device of forgetfulness or a compensation for neglect. The vision assailed me quite sharply of a casual disaster. It was a late August day, when the Mistral makes the sea unusually rough. At one moment the child of nature was on the rocks, and then was not there. What strange vague hostility caused my consciousness's momentary but crucial delay? There was time to stand up, to look, to search, to initiate a rescue. But it was my contentment to continue writing in my book. I did nothing.

And now the rocks were empty, and might always have been empty. I myself stayed only to finish what

39

I was writing. Later the old fishermen would come with their black rods and crumbled bread in the lids of Camembert boxes. I had seen them often, standing at the edge of the rocks in the swirling foam, wearing old trunks rolled half-way up one buttock. They had their own dignity of a sort.

The Party

They found her crying by herself in Jeremy's study. She was seated at the desk in front of the telephone, as though she had put down the receiver after hearing bad news. Her feet hung down over the chair in their white socks and new red party shoes with the single button, ten inches above the carpet. She looked up at them through the single tear that lined her face like a snail-track, and her face bestowed on them that helpless rueful smile she had recently learned, the one that admitted that her behaviour was impossible but made an immediate appeal for forgiveness and understanding.

'Why on earth are you in here, pooch?' said Olivia. 'What's the matter?'

A fly grumbled in the window pane, trying without much conviction to escape from an old corner of web. Because of his Argentinian trip, Jeremy hadn't been in his study much that summer. Dust sparkled in a shaft of sunlight that fell on the desk. From the garden came the sound of children playing.

'Your guests are enjoying themselves no end,' said

Jeremy, picking up a tax voucher from his desk and looking at it without great curiosity. He put it back and gave her a ready smile.

'The sausages are done,' said Olivia. 'I was just going to take them outside, but Daddy said you'd disappeared. He's got a new game to play. You'll have to pick a team, you see. But suddenly you weren't there.'

'No, I wasn't, was I!' agreed Lucy with a laugh that had a little breathless lift to it as she recovered from her weeping. 'I wasn't there!'

'Why not, darling?' said her mother. 'Aren't you enjoying yourself?'

'Oh yes,' said Lucy emphatically. 'Yes, I am. Very much.'

'Well then,' said Olivia. 'What's up?'

'You gave me the impression,' said Jeremy, 'of quite looking forward to this party. Have we talked about anything else for the last month? I doubt that we have. You even invited Tony Perkins.'

Lucy gave another little tearful laugh.

'And only last night,' he continued, turning to the window and looking out over the Ch. de clos Vougeot at the scene of enjoyment, 'I heard you telling Mr Floppisides, and Plunger, and Duck, that you were so very much looking forward to it.'

'Yes,' said Lucy. 'Yes.'

'And Mummy has quite excelled herself in the kitchen,' he said. 'I have seen jam sandwiches as thin as the ace of hearts, and cider in real champagne bottles if I'm not mistaken, and there are jellies. Oh my God, are there jellies! They're like the Crown Jewels. You can tolerate jellies, can't you?'

Lucy nodded vigorously.

'So what's up, pooch?' asked her mother.

'Well you see, Mummy,' said Lucy, staring hard at her knees and looking up at them earnestly. 'You see, the little hand's here, isn't it, and the big hand is *here*, down here.' She pointed to the coloured nodding surface of her wristwatch. 'That means it's past half past four o'clock already.'

'Time and tide wait for no man,' said Jeremy.

'And that means,' said Lucy, 'that it's half over. It's more than half over.'

'But darling,' said Olivia, 'there's lots of it left. The best part is left.'

Lucy looked from one to the other, happy successful parents who loved her and who didn't understand, and another wave of panic surged in her mind.

'No,' she sobbed, turning away from them. 'I mean it's happening. It's all happening. It's really happened now. It's over. It's over.'

Applecheek Woods

We'd been looking forward to our trip to Applecheek Woods for weeks. There were notes to take home about the money for the coach, and about bringing sandwiches. We had to get up really early, so the sandwiches had to be made the night before. Maureen Philips ate hers while we were still outside the school gates waiting for the coach. She said she hadn't had any breakfast. Miss Govette said she was a silly girl, and what would she do for lunch? Maureen sulked, and when we all climbed in she ran off home, saying she wasn't going to miss her dinner.

Everyone wanted to sit next to Wayne because of the Spitfire. They were all going to want to have a go. I didn't bother too much about it because I'd helped him more than anyone and knew that I could have lots of turns. Little Billy Wilson was sick out of the window and had to go and sit with Miss Govette. When we arrived at Applecheek Woods the streak of sick was still there on the side of the coach.

Miss Govette's idea was that we would bring the things we had made in our handiwork class and make

44

use of them. We had all groaned and collapsed about and slammed our desk-lids when she announced this, but she had stood before us with her staring eyes and big smile and just kept her hands in the air and shouted us down. It was her big plan. That was all right for the girls, who had all made baskets. They were going to pick blackberries and crab-apples and wild plums which they could then make jam with. Some of us had made shoebags out of a big roll of coloured deckchair material, and we were supposed to bring our sandwiches in them. They looked a bit daft, though, and we left them in the coach. Colin had insisted on making something really useful, but he could hardly have brought a pair of book-ends to Applecheek Woods, could he? Miss Govette made him carry her hold-all.

I should have known that it would be difficult to get near the Spitfire. It looked so strange, being finished. Smaller than I thought it would be. But it still had that wonderful smell of balsa cement. The only thing I knew like it was the nail varnish that my sister Monica put on the ends of her fingers. I didn't see why it didn't stick them together, like it did the wing-struts of the Spitfire. But I suppose it wasn't the same sort of stuff, really. Tony Moffatt was fussing about it, and pushing his way forward. I got fed up, and when the tail got broken I went away by myself. They were all gathered around, and Wayne was pretending that he could mend it, but I knew better.

It was boring in Applecheek Woods. I might have joined the girls and picked blackberries, but I didn't have a basket. I was one of those who had made a shoe-bag. It was typical of Wayne to get away with bringing his Spitfire. I suppose you could call it handi-work, but he hadn't made it at school.

I walked off for miles until I was entirely by myself. I ate my sandwiches, and it didn't give me much satisfaction that I'd put into them some tinned salmon that my sister Monica had been saving for herself. I didn't really like tinned salmon.

It was warm, and I must have been going around in circles. I picked a red toadstool with white spots on it which I thought Miss Govette was bound to be interested in. She was always going on about nature. I came down out of the bit of wood I was in, and found I was on the edge of a clearing. Who should I see but Miss Govette herself, lying back in the sun in that small quiet place, with her eyes closed. It was funny to find her there, because I thought I'd walked right away from everyone. I was about to call out: 'Hallo, Miss!', when I suddenly knew I shouldn't do. Something was wrong.

Was she in pain?

I knew that people had fits. Mrs Cooper's Stuart had fits. He fell back on the floor and made strange noises. Was Miss Govette having a fit?

In the same instant, when I saw her feet stretched out I saw two other feet sticking out from her flowery skirt. It was as though she had four feet: two of her own, with bare feet, because she must have kicked off her shoes, and two other smaller ones in yellow socks and blue-sided trainers. I couldn't believe what I saw. It was one of us, one of the children, down in there. I felt sick and excited, and in the stillness my heart was thudding as though I were the only real thing in the world. As though it were me down there moving curiously and busily inside the skirt like a collapsed tent.

I knew that when we were all gathered in the car-park again and the driver had the coach engine purring ready to go I could play detective and look for yellow socks and blue-sided trainers. But at the same time I somehow knew that the identification wouldn't solve the mystery. I wasn't even sure what the mystery itself was, though I knew that nothing else I had ever experienced had made me feel so completely alone, and restless at being alone. It was most like seeing Tony Moffatt fiddling with the damaged tail of the Spitfire and making it worse rather than better, and I also thought of my sister Monica ready to go out in the evening, turning round and round to show me how her skirt opened and closed as it swirled one way and another, and her fingers smelling of balsa cement, and the smell of her knickers in the bathroom.

The Space around the Child

It was wonderful to see Margot again after all those years. Hang on a minute. No, it wasn't actually. I had *thought* it would be, that was the thing, and right up to the moment I entered her loft apartment on the Lower East Side I was remembering all the things that were vaguely exciting about her. I remembered an evening on the river at Oxford with her and Tony and Gill and the bats flickering among the pollarded willows and she saying (in that considered way she had that made everyone ponder and then talk about something else): 'Loneliness is nothing but the ability to imagine other people's lives.' I remembered her rather severe little nose, like a pale equilateral triangle. I remembered someone talking in admiring terms about her work on the philosophy of the Future. It had to be explained to me that this wasn't the radical reassessment of the whole of philosophy that it sounded as if it might be, a sort of prophetic glimpse of a feminist millennium, but serious work on our fallacious concept of what the 'future' might actually be. It was to do with identity, awareness of the self, and so on.

'Did you ever finish your thesis?' I asked her, when we were settled with large vodkas and orange-juice in the one area of the rambling and museum-like apartment that appeared to be designed for comfort and conversation, but only just.

'Of course not,' said Margot. 'My supervisor stole all my best ideas. Isn't that what graduate students are for? To help their supervisors hold down the jobs that should by rights be passed on to them?'

I went through the motions of concern. Wasn't there something she could have done about it?

'I was amused at first,' she said. 'But there were better things to do. I had a child to bring up, after all.'

More motions of concern. Though from all I had heard, any element of accident or abandonment in Margot's role as a single parent had long been overtaken by her occupational enthusiasm for it. Little Sarah's father had receded into the anonymity of some obscure historical episode. And Margot had theories about child-rearing that she held as tenaciously as her propositions in philosophy. In fact, Sarah had taken the place of her thesis.

'I don't think parents ever realise,' said Margot, 'the importance of the space around a child.'

This made me think of the space around Margot. There were little piles of the right books, office lighting, glassware that had never been wet. I suppose as

49

students we can never afford to live in the style we have in mind, but knowing Margot's mind I perhaps should have been prepared for this.

'We get used to people invading our privacy,' she went on, 'precisely because of this violation of personal space in infancy. There's a poet (is it Frost?) who said: "The frontier of my person goes, some thirty inches from my nose." Not enough, in my book! Still, it's a beginning.'

'I thought children needed hugging,' I said, wondering if Margot needed hugging, and if I would myself want to do the hugging.

'It's absolutely what they *don't* want,' said Margot, crossing her legs and placing her left elbow and wrist along the arm of her chair as though in preparation for it to be manacled there. With her right hand she tossed the remains of her vodka down her throat and looked across her nose at me in the way she had. 'It suffocates them. It saps their will-power. Don't you think?'

I didn't know what to think. Hugging, in Margot's 'book', was some kind of outmoded fallacy, probably worthy of a brief but vicious appendix. And perhaps, too, she had been right at Oxford about the future. Perhaps it was best to expect nothing from it, to have no relations with it at all, to abolish the whole concept, like hugging. Whatever I had expected from looking Margot up was pretty rapidly evaporating.

Before Margot could ask me about my own life,

though I doubt she was interested enough to do so with more than perfunctory politeness, Sarah herself came into the room, announcing that it was time for her to watch TV.

'Hi,' I said, though we had not been introduced.

She took no notice of me at all, but turned on the set and sat expectantly in front of it, with a kind of pleasureless intentness, as though she had just that minute used up all her life-skills and needed some official instructions as to how to manage to get through the rest of the day. As the room began to fill with the dopey cartoon music, Margot smiled at me and shrugged. There was no complicity in it, however, no allusion to any possible escape from this intrusion. It was a pleasant enough gesture, but it had the air of a not even particularly reluctant farewell.

Maybe I should have been impressed by the degree of domestic competence all this revealed. The child was neatly dressed, quiet, well nourished. The apartment was impressive in its way. It made its effect without speaking particularly of money. Margot had all the sexual confidence of still being on the right side of thirty.

But something had been unwittingly given away. There was a barrier I was not being invited to cross. Perhaps, belonging to the past, I could never also belong to the future. We made some vague arrangement that both of us knew we need not keep.

My last sight of Sarah was of her dignified little

profile bathed in the moving colours of the television. She seemed to know that her life was perfectly ordained. She sat there, confident of both the present and the future, with the graceful rapt smile of a madonna, unhugged, with her mother's beautiful nose.

Someone's Brother

The door opened a crack, then widened to a hardly more sociable foot. The woman looked up at them with neither hostility nor welcome.

'It's me again,' said his sister brightly.

The woman let them in, without speaking. She looked briefly from one to the other before leading them into the untidy kitchen. His sister's reassurances had been correct: the woman didn't ask who he was, and took no notice of him from then on. To her he was just someone who came with the visit. He hadn't come last time, and might not come next time. If he had business of his own, he would bring it up sooner or later. She wasn't going to make extra trouble by asking him.

He was staying with his sister because he had nowhere else to stay, and he was accompanying her on her visits because he had nothing better to do. He didn't ask what they were about. He wasn't even sure quite what it was his sister did. He didn't know the woman's name.

She had two children. One was a stout toddler wear-

53

ing only a jersey. His penis, like a frond of bladder-wrack lifted by the tide, shook as he stomped around the kitchen thrusting his feeding-cup into his mouth. The snot had dribbled and clustered from his nose like the wax down a chianti bottle in a cheap Italian restaurant. Strands of it caught on the spout of the feeding cup and were lifted away like melted cheese.

The other was a little girl who should have been at school and was clearly bored. While his sister talked to the woman the girl came over and took both his hands, as if to make him get up and play. She was pale, silent and insistent, shaking a lock of fair hair from her eyes, pulling him up. He preferred sitting where he was, where he would be least noticed.

'What have you been drawing?' he whispered, resisting the pull of her hands. Perhaps she would bring him her drawing-book and they could look at it quietly together. She didn't respond, but became more interested in his resisting hands. As he tried to escape her cupped grip she caught his thumbs and wouldn't let them go. She straddled his bent knee as though to ride it, using his thumbs as though they were the horns of a wild steer. Her skirt rode up, revealing the greyish pants stretched tightly but incompletely over the clefted groin which she had placed precisely on his kneecap. He could feel her whole pelvic bone fitting it like a socket. She released one of his thumbs just for a moment and rearranged her skirt so that it decorously hid her bony saddle. Then she grabbed the thumb again quickly before it had time to move away, and began to ride her steer.

His knee was crooked over the other, so he couldn't move it. He had no means of slowing or restraining her rocking movement. If he withdrew his hands, or moved them apart, this merely improved the game, challenging her to hang on and keep her balance while the unwilling and motionless steer beneath her caused her to buck wildly.

All the time she stared into his face casually, deliberately, but with no air of challenge. She was absorbed but quite indifferent to his feelings.

Did the mother not see it? His sister was in the middle of a difficult explanation, and was perhaps grateful to him for keeping the child occupied. The toddler was banging his feeding bottle against a chair leg. No one was paying any attention. No one had names. He felt himself losing his will as the girl stared him down.

Did they not notice that he was being molested?

Report on the Planet

Although it seems barely credible, I have to report that, contrary to what I may have previously indicated, the inhabitants of this planet are unlike us in more important respects than mere size, destiny, means of locomotion and so on, the characteristics that I hope you are by now familiar with and which I hope have helped you to comprehend their strangeness.

The most significant new difference which I have discovered concerns their impermanence. Do you understand the principle of impermanence? It was postulated some years ago as a direction which organic life might have taken under unfavourable circumstances, but of course it was never imagined that in some obscure corner of the universe such conditions might actually obtain. I never read all the literature on the subject, since much of it was too technical (and of course quite hypothetical), but I remember a few facts. It's very exciting to have discovered real examples of this state of things in living beings, albeit so entirely primitive.

You will know even less of the theory than I do, so how can I explain? It appears that their bodies at some stage do not exist at all and have to come into being. I can imagine the scepticism with which you will read this, but it is true! And then, having come into being, they change in various ways. Change in shape and appearance, I mean. Not like the gases and liquids of their planet (which behave in ways not unlike our own, though at vastly different temperatures) but much more slowly and hardly to be observed as they occur by any of the senses, mine or theirs, it would seem. These changes are known as development. This apparently follows natural laws which are grudgingly accepted by all who undergo it, and to which as far as I can see there are no exceptions not even among the most powerful or intelligent of the race.

These mysteriously created beings are in full possession of the knowledge and wisdom appropriate to the conduct of life, as you might expect. Care is taken of them in secluded areas of the community, and assistance given in matters of bodily function, perambulation and so on. How they are created I have no idea as yet, though it seems that some of them appear out of fire or are found in the ground in long boxes.

But from that moment onwards this strange 'development' occurs. They become more active and confident, their bodily surface acquires greater colour, their movements become quicker, their behaviour towards each other less considerate.

You will understand how difficult it is for me to observe these beings properly without giving myself away. My information is scant, my generalisations necessarily based on rather few individual cases.

What happens next in this development, you will ask? I'm afraid that I find this part of my account painful to transmit. It may be that we ourselves could tolerate impermanence of some kind if at some pre-determined moment we simply ceased to exist. If it were a question of appearing and disappearing, and perhaps knowing nothing much about it.

It is not like that for the inhabitants of this planet. They dwindle, and become ignorant and foolish. Their energy becomes concentrated, their vigour expended upon trivialities. They seem to have little knowledge and become satisfied with crude bright objects that make simple noises.

And the ultimate destiny of these beings is painful to contemplate. After many efforts I have managed to observe one of them in a state as close to non-being as makes no difference. It was tended in secret, away from all the others, so that they did not have to observe its torment. It had shrunk to a painfully small size, and was absolutely helpless. The reddened wrinkled body was being doused in liquids to soothe its surface and to calm its frantic agonised movements.

I have occasionally heard them talk of this process of non-being. It is called death.

I do not think I can admire the life of this planet,

though of course its natural inhabitants must endure it. I shall continue to observe them, and send in my reports.

III

YESTERDAY'S DREAMS

Romance

James has been complaining almost every day. It's as though out of sheer perversity he would have liked it to be a kind of honeymoon after all. 'Can't we rest? We've been tramping all day, all these chateaux.' I thought it was rather clever of me not to get simply furious. Now I'm worried. He just hasn't got any energy.

I don't expect much. Nothing very interesting is going to happen. If an Angevin prince in a blue steel haubergeon comes galloping over the dusty bridge, he doesn't look at me. He might lift the little bugle that's slung on a baldric at his waist, and emit some graceful alarm, faltering slightly as he bumps along with the horse's motion. But I'm not involved. It's just a story that might have happened.

The reality is that manufacturer's wife from Poitiers, the tartan beret and slightly chewing jaw. It's the stern gaze down the fairway and the heavy husband always a length behind. Might as well be her caddy. Ugh.

You can't blame them for turning over the grounds to expensive sports, but it makes it more of a crush than it need be. I can almost understand James's reluctance to stand in line for a glimpse of historical episodes lurking in unreadable deeds of title or moth-eaten wall hangings. You can get a better tea in Hindhead.

Well, it was James who wanted to do all this, wasn't it? I want romance. Let's leave the Loire behind: foot down on the accelerator, heading for Pyla-sur-Mer and the Atlantic breakers. But after a while he makes me drive. His sandals are uncomfortable.

On the beach he sleeps, and I can pretend that he has heroic shoulders. I doze as well, sinking mindlessly into the sounds of the afternoon, the drone of a bi-plane, the tiny shouts of children. I sleep in the heat, but really I want to dance in the waves that crash on the beach.

I wake to hear James moaning. Reaching over to calm him, I notice the white shoelaces loose over his heels. But of course he isn't wearing shoes. The laces stir. They are flat worms waving from the cracks in his heels where he has been walking in his sandals. The soles of his feet are crammed with these worms, coiled tightly like the inside of a golf-ball. He's been walking on them all day, and the pressure is forcing them out, splitting the sole of his foot.

Poor James. Why am I not more disgusted? It simply seems pathetic, like an involuntary display of some inner lack. As if every gallantry had come down to this.

He sleepily asks me what the matter is. I want to pull them out without telling him, but I know there are too many. I use the corner of the beach towel to take hold of them, trying to tease them out. They break off, in little segments. They seem to become enraged and seethe, distorting the shape of the ball of his heel.

Soon the whole sole of the foot is loose like the flap of a tramp's boot.

I think: he didn't really want me after all, he never wanted to come, and all the time we were admiring those fairy turrets, that grey-violet stone, the dungeons, he was walking about on *these*.

Rules

We were throwing stones on the beach, trying to hit a yellow rusting oil-can on top of which were balanced other stones. A resounding clump against the can was good, even if achieved by a lucky ricochet. Dislodging a balanced stone was even better. And we were telling dreams.

The dreams didn't matter any more than the throwing of the stones. They were both activities induced by unusual idleness. Everyone had slept on and on, waking by chance, perhaps at a stray noise, or simply from the sense that it was unduly late. Dreams were therefore remembered, and therefore related.

'I was with Sven in a sort of dormobile,' said Margaret. 'And there was a body to dispose of.'

Everyone cheered.

'His, presumably,' said David, throwing two stones at once. He sounded perfectly ready to accept Margaret's dream. Perhaps he had heard it already, and knew that it was safe for public consumption. Or perhaps he knew instinctively how far she would go before censoring it.

Sven hadn't joined in the stone-throwing. He was playing his guitar without ever quite embarking on any particular tune.

'Not his,' said Alicia. 'His murdered guitar's. You couldn't stand the guitar, Margaret, so you did it in.'

'Poor guitar,' said Sven softly, stroking it.

Olly hit the oil-can, and everyone cheered again. He went to replace the fallen stones, and when he came back he announced: 'The guitar is a symbol of the female.'

'Oh yes?' said Alicia suspiciously.

'Of course,' said Olly. 'You only have to look at it.'

'Everything is a symbol of something else in a dream,' said Sven. 'Margaret's dream probably wasn't about me at all.'

'Exactly,' said Olly. 'It was probably about Alicia.'

So we drivelled on. I wondered why we should be so content to analyse dreams in this way when we would have been embarrassed to have analysed real relationships. It was just a game. Like hitting the oil-can. Dreams themselves were just games, and perhaps symbolism did provide rules of a sort. Of course, they were immensely more complex than any rules of interpretation we cared to obey, and we knew it. As far as we were at all interested in recounting the dreams we used it merely as a cover for pleasantries. It was something to do.

Rather a waste of time, really. I would rather have

been finding out more about Alicia. I quite wanted to know just what had happened to Olly's brother. And I could do without the self-satisfied Sven. But there seemed to be different rules for our behaviour when we were all together than those for any smaller combinations of us.

I suppose that even these rules belonged to nature. Groups of things behave in certain ways, and that was as true of the six of us as of the millions of water molecules that made up the cloud that was drifting above our heads at that moment. Or, more appositely, of the pebbles in the little bay where we had wandered. I said so.

'All we're doing is moving these stones from one part of the beach to another,' I said. 'The sea does that anyway.'

'Some of us rather more quickly than others,' said Margaret. 'David, really!'

David was now throwing stones by the handful.

'Yes,' said Olly. 'You're cheating.'

'I'm allowed to do this,' said David, 'because I didn't have any dreams at all.'

'That's your own fault,' said Sven. 'Only people who are either perfectly happy or perfectly boring don't have dreams. Which are you, David?'

'Yes, darling,' said Margaret. 'Go on, tell us which you are.'

The cloud above us continued its large unfurling, and the sea below us continued its sullen process of turning large pebbles into smaller pebbles and smaller pebbles into sand. And our minds became weary of dreams as did our arms of throwing stones, for we were not perfectly anything much at all, and had made up all the rules ourselves.

The Dark Girl

The crisis, if it was indeed a crisis, seemed to elude us all. We weren't sure if we had witnessed it or not. Or even if it had occurred. Perhaps it was something to do with the sun, which was out unfailingly every morning, hot on the paths, on the stone sills and stoups of the staircases, ready to make us blink, and grin as we stumbled out to breakfast, shouting: 'Hey, what d'ya know? Where's all this rain they told us about?'

In the Lodge the Porters behaved as though they had twice as many secrets as usual to keep. It's the way the English have. They aren't telling you anything, but they want you to know it. When I asked for the squash-court keys that very prim one looked at me from under the lids of his eyes and asked me if I had heard anything during the night.

'No,' I said, 'I didn't hear anything. What kind of thing should I have heard?'

Not to worry, he says. He wasn't saying as how I should have heard anything in particular, and if I didn't hear anything then so much the better.

'Was it a break-in?' I asked.

Nothing like that, he says.

'Someone in trouble?' I asked.

Something like that, he says. But he'd only come on duty that morning and he didn't rightly know. And he pursed his lips in that deliberate way he had, like a judge, and gave me the keys. I knew I wouldn't get any more out of him. I didn't even know whether he wanted me to, I mean, or whether he was trying to get something out of me. Some of the other fellows played him up a lot and he seemed to like it. He was a great snob. But he didn't seem to like me much.

I was just going to knock around by myself for a while. I didn't have anyone to play with. So when I saw Charlie talking in the front quad with a couple of the best-looking girls on the summer school, I went up to them and passed the time of day. I thought I might just get a game from one of them, and if I didn't, then what matter?

We were just standing about as everybody does. The more talkative of the girls kept laughing and looking at her feet. She had a really neat nose and jaw and a very freckled face. She was complaining about one of the courses, but in a very mild sort of way, and I noticed that she kept looking up at Charlie to see if he was still interested in what she was saying.

Charlie was interested all right. He nodded all the time, and grinned, and kept taking little steps backward and then forward again, and hitching up the back of his baggy shorts.

'Hey, Charlie,' I said. 'Did something happen last night? Everyone's talking about it.'

'Talking about what?' said Charlie.

'I don't know,' I admitted. 'Did any of you guys hear anything?'

The freckled girl shook her head and stared at her feet again. The dark one was smiling. She had been smiling all the time, clutching her A4 pad in front of her in an odd sort of way, her arms crossed in front so that she was gripping it from opposite ends. I suddenly saw the force of that grip. And the smile, too, was like a kind of grip.

'Some of the fellows were having a lot of fun,' said Charlie. 'I think they were going on a raid of one of the girls' staircases. Is that what you're talking about? Some weirdo dyke there apparently. Sonny Bauer claimed she wore Y-fronts. Me, I turned in early. I mean, I've got better things to do. Like, take sex. Take sex itself, in its essence. I don't suppose . . .'

'Shut up, Charlie,' I said.

'Don't tell me to shut up,' protested Charlie, with a laugh.

'Shut *up*,' I insisted.

The dark girl was still smiling, but her eyes were fixed somewhere else, on nothing, or on terror. She was standing there (how long had she been standing?) rooted in absolute terror. And still smiling.

Fancy

What do they want, the ones who don't want it? What's their secret? He's not bent, he's bloody married. His daughter's older than me. Even she's married. How do you get into that safe little world, all those interlocking pieces, everyone relating to everyone else and the picture just like it is on the box, even bigger? I think I must be meant not to fit in. I'm the missing piece of edge.

He's not gorgeous. I mean he's too old to be gorgeous. But when he comes out of his office you can feel it. You don't even have to look up. Gail's desk faces the other way, and she said she can feel it. The atmosphere completely changes. It's as though he sets us all humming. You're sitting there with this letter to Craig Harwood and Souter or whatever, and you know he's in the room. It's as though you've slowed up. You hear the thud of each key. The carriage return sounds like an arrow going into your throat. And there's this inaudible collective humming from down there between our legs. It's incredible. He's like Pavarotti setting wine glasses off. You can feel the reverberation running up your whole body.

And he's very friendly. He's not at all like the others. You can talk to him and he really seems to listen. And he doesn't give you any unnecessary work. If you make a mistake he'll just correct it himself. He won't go on about it. And he comes to the *Dog and Trumpet* and buys his round, too. But then he always goes home.

I went to Ealing one weekend, to see his house. I went by tube, and walked for ages through these leafy streets, getting lost. I felt such a fool. I mean, I might have been noticed. I stood on the other side of the road and could see his wife moving about in the front room. It gave me a shock. She was this old woman, really quite old, older than my mother.

How do you tell someone like that you fancy them? How do you even introduce the subject? I told him about Steve, to see if that got him interested. It's a good ploy. You can usually tell if it does, if they are interested, that is. You can see this sort of wave pass over their faces, a kind of slight freeze. Then you know. You know they don't like to hear about the competition. They'll do something then that'll give themselves away, even if it's just something like leaning forward. They'll lean towards you. It's a giveaway. It's pure jealousy.

With him I couldn't decide one way or the other. He hadn't gone home yet that evening, and we were alone in the pub. That seemed significant enough. Why did he stay? He once said it was a way of beating the rush-hour: you could leave an hour later and still get home at the same time. But he didn't have to spend his time with us, did he?

He was polite about Steve, asked questions. But I put it down to his icy self-control. There he was, after all, just me and him. He had to be interested!

Then I had this idea of suggesting that he came swimming in the lunch break. I used to go with Gail sometimes. You paid the earth, but it was worth it. I had this new two-piece costume in black and emerald, cut really high on the hip. The material had a geometric design: interlocking triangles that all seemed to lead in one direction. I really wanted him to see me in that. Just thinking of it made me feel quite faint.

He was polite about that, too. He said what a good thing it was for someone of his age. It prevented flab.

But he hasn't come yet. I mentioned it again, but I can't go on about it. I don't get that many chances. He won't come, of course. Did I scare him off?

It's murder. I can bring myself off within two minutes just sitting at my desk, flexing my thighs. I can time it for when he's in the room. Life is simply draining away. There's nothing left for me. I shall be twenty in a few months.

The Man I Love

Logicians tell us that before you can use any rule you have to have a rule which tells you how to use that rule. Hold that in your head for a minute. Now think about the man I love: he's thirty-six and losing his hair a bit, but wears it neat and short to make the most of it; he doesn't drink; he's in the Inland Revenue but wears an olive Gap tee-shirt; he reads Sara Paretsky and Iain Banks, and has this slightly surprised expression on his face that I've noticed lots of very tall people have. You won't want me to go on. By the way, I'm much younger and quite good-looking, luckily, good enough to work in the cosmetics departments of Debenhams anyway. No problem about catching admiring glances.

But did I say there was a problem? If you're philosophical about these things you have to admit that you can hardly fall in love with people you've never met. But I've never seen that as a reason for not falling in love with someone you do meet, just because you might never have met them or (more usually) because you might meet someone else. People who argue like that, people like Jane Brewster, can't ever have experienced the real thing. Everything they say sounds so theoretical, even if it might be true.

Take the rule business. If that was true, then no one could speak to each other at all. Not only would I not know that he likes reading Sara Paretsky, he wouldn't be able to read Sara Paretsky in the first place. You'd need a language in which to explain that language, and so on. You'd never get started. That's what I meant. If people like Jane Brewster were right, you'd never get started. Take true love. That sounds like a cheap magazine, but you know what I mean. How do you know it's going to be the real thing? How do you know it's going to last a lifetime? You don't know that until the lifetime's over, till death us do part. Then you'd know it had been, and that's marvellous, but you can't wait that long before beginning, can you?

My mother's always going on about rules. 'Never marry the first man you fall in love with,' she'll say, as though men are pubs you're thinking of stopping for lunch at. It's hardly a rule you can live by, is it? That's not what love is. If you couldn't marry the first man you fell in love with you'd be pretty careful not to let yourself fall in love, wouldn't you? If you were beginning to care, that is. So you'd never begin, because you'd know it couldn't come to anything. So you'd never marry. 'Mum,' I'll ask her. 'What about you and Dad?' 'What about it?' she'll say. 'It must mean you loved men before him,' I'll say. And she'll blush and say: 'Well, you couldn't call that being in love,' and I'll reply: 'Then Dad was the first man you were in love with and according to you you shouldn't have married him.' She's got nothing to say then, and I feel awful. I might just as well be Jane Brewster. So I give her a hug, and it's all right.

So I go by feelings not rules. My feelings tell me that he's the man for me. If I had rules I might easily have said that I didn't want a very tall man. I'm quite petite myself. But there you are, you see. My only rule is that there shouldn't be any rules.

I can understand Mum in a way. In theory you can always imagine something better. But when you *know* it's right you don't ever want to risk losing it. The man I love is the most precious thing in the world to me. I'm terrified of losing him. Mum would understand that, surely? It can't be wrong. It can't.

So I think I'll get my glass filled up and go over and see if he'll talk to me again.

Toasting the Crust

I'm using up my dreams, she thought. I'm using them up too quickly. If I could have them again, I would. I'd save them. But as it is, I lose them the moment I wake up. I might just as well never have them.

She pulled her upper lip savagely down over her teeth and dabbed round her nose with lotion. She might have been trying to rub it off. Well, it gave her no pleasure, and it wasn't just the greasiness. It had the air of unnecessary shape, this nose, the merest over-elaboration, like an armchair with wings. It was too dignified, as noses went.

The loaf was whole, but not fresh. That was because yesterday she had still been finishing the previous one. She cut off the crust and one thick slice which she put under the grill. Then she put the crust under the grill as well.

I needn't eat it, she thought. I won't eat it. But I know I'm going to, or I wouldn't have toasted it. Why do I have to eat everything up? I'm always a loaf behind. I'm always using stale bread. Perhaps it's like

79

that with dreams. Perhaps I'm using up yesterday's dreams.

In that case, what becomes of today's dreams? I suppose I can never have them at all, like Alice's jam. It's one way of saving them.

Marmite with the crust and marmalade with the slice? Or marmite with the slice and marmalade with the crust? There was no one to observe her choice and judge the significance of either banquet. She imagined what Mr Sherwin would think. The nub of the matter was the deliberate demoting of the preferred, the confining of a small indulgence. But Mr Sherwin's tastes, even if she could be sure of guessing them correctly, could not possibly help her with her own. And was she confident of knowing her own? No, she was not. She would have to consider the rival attractions in a purer form, as though both pieces of toast had to be spread from the same jar. She saw Mr Sherwin in her mind's eye unscrewing each lid in turn, sniffing, and tilting the jars as if to see how much of each had already been consumed.

She had never, to her knowledge, dreamed of Mr Sherwin, though she had often wished to. You can't make yourself dream of particular things, can you? It would hardly be fair. You could construct an entirely desirable alternative life, and there would never be any inducement to get out of bed at all. Suppose you could think of the various elements beforehand: a warm day, by the beach; the ability to run, the calf muscles rippling in slow motion; air dividing on either side of the nose, a *perfect* demonstration like a Silver Cloud; Mr Sherwin smiling, loosening his striped tie; piles of fruit. Quite beautiful, perfectly irresponsible, altogether impossible.

With her finger on the nozzle, she released the scent of pine forests into the room. It always gave her a little shiver, as though something of herself had escaped into the air. That was because the contents of the can were finite, like life itself. Each little touch, so authentic, so redolent of itself, brought you closer to the end. You didn't want to waste it, but there was nothing to save it for. It had to be used.

Now she was quite ready. Everything was in order. She was clean. The day seemed to be just like any other. She was ready for Mr Sherwin.

Sunday Morning

You can only play God with other lives than your own. Those are the rules. Look at that blackbird greedily eyeing the bushes. It's after the robin's nest again. Didn't you know that birds eat birds? What's the difference, do you think, between the rubbery slobber of an unhoused snail and a tempting twiggy dish of nude fledglings? Not much. Except that one is rather harder to get than the other.

Nests are easy. Malcolm is into nests, any nest but his own. Like an irresponsible god, his libido a great cupboard of disguises. He'd have to pretend, wouldn't he? You don't expect a Malcolm to risk anything. You don't expect a Malcolm to have desires. Malcolm is scout-tags on socks. Malcolm is checking the oil and water. Malcolm is closing the little cardboard lip on the cereal packet.

Not my Malcolm. My Malcolm has brown, beautiful eyes, deep and devious as the vacant unblinking lens of the blackbird, always staring away, to the side, even apparently behind, as though it had no intentions about anything at all. Pure evil. Then off like a bullet into the bay tree, scrabbling in the leaves for its greedy pleasure.

What did Juno think about, I wonder, creaking irritably in her striped golden chair throughout her long day of rest? The newspaper may be half an inch thick, but it comes to an end soon enough. The third cup of coffee tastes like metal. The sun goes behind a cloud. Probably to do secret and terrible things. Like Jupiter.

Get out of it, blackbird! Away with you. Lead your own life.

Does Malcolm fancy me lounging here in my deshabille with an image of him teeing off virtuously at the fifth with Harry Chapman? Crouching on the emerald grass for a putt, with one little clenched black-gloved hand, like Dr Strangelove? Easy enough to imagine all that ritual, I dare say, but the truth is that he doesn't fancy *me* at all. It's Glenys Chapman that he fancies. What a farce.

Except that if it really was a farce, like a stage set with seven or eight doors, then at this moment Harry Chapman would be here, with me, and never mind the deshabille. I can't say I'd care for that, thank you very much. So where does it leave me?

It leaves me quite unconcerned, really. It leaves me not actually caring very much. Like God, I suppose, who seems to have created the world in a moment of boredom when he didn't have anything better to do, and then forgot all about it. That accounts for the infinite tedium of Sunday, pure disgust at the meaninglessness of it all.

I don't know why we go on with it, I really don't. There's always fresh ice in the ice-tray. There's always a rosemary-sprigged roast ready to pop into the oven. There's always the hope that the sun will come out again. And I shall never say anything to Malcolm, never ask the right question, the awkward question. And it'll be the same next year as it was last year and the birds will go on constructing their idiot nests. And there'll always be a Glenys Chapman.

No you don't, Mr Blackbird! At least I can dispense some justice around here. Out you come. Be off with you.

Oh dear. What a boo-boo. But I might have known it. It's what comes of playing God. God started it with the biggest mistake of all, so it's no wonder mistakes go on being made. The robin's nest isn't the robin's nest at all. It's the blackbird's nest.

I think perhaps there's one section of the paper that I haven't looked at yet.

IV

THE WORLD OF COLONEL ABU

The Impossible Execution

When the news reached his prison cell that they were each to be summarily executed on some unspecified date before Ramadan, the barber Mehdi was outraged.

'How can Colonel Abu do this to me?' he said to his cell-mates. 'He knows I'm innocent.'

But his cell-mates, who were guilty and knew they were guilty, merely shrugged. One of them, it is true, started to pray, but the other two went on playing cards. They knew that there was nothing they could do about it. They were resigned to death.

Mehdi paced about the cell in a fury. It was only his anger at the great injustice that was being done to him that prevented him from being terrified. The others openly admitted that they had been involved in an attempt on Colonel's Abu's life. The bomb had failed to go off, and they had been traced to Mehdi's shop, where they were all arrested. They had stood there in handcuffs, their chins still fragrant with foam, grinning proudly while the photographers took their pictures. And poor Mehdi had been arrested along with them.

The guards laughed at his tears of rage.

'Go ahead,' they said. 'Kick the wall all you want. There's nothing you can do about it. The day will come when you least expect it. It's the way the Colonel likes to do it. Then you'll be pissing yourself with fear.'

Mehdi was a cunning man, even though he was only a barber. He thought about what the guards had said, and the next time they came to laugh at him he presented to them a face of imperturbable calm and frank amusement.

Intrigued and irritated, they asked him what had caused this change of attitude. Mehdi replied that he knew for certain that Colonel Abu would be unable to carry out his threat, and that therefore he had nothing to fear. And as if to prove it he whistled a few bars of a popular song called 'Feed me with figs and I am yours for ever.'

The next day the first of the terrorists was taken away and executed. The guards expected Mehdi to show signs of anger or fear but he seemed to be quite unaffected. One by one all his cell-mates were shot, but when the guards came to gloat over the barber, now the last man in the cell, they found him singing 'Feed me with figs' in full voice, and performing a little dance into the bargain.

They were quite amazed, and being superstitious men asked him to explain to them why he was so confident that he would not die.

'I will certainly do so,' said Mehdi. 'For has not Allah said that wisdom may be given even to the humble? And is it not true that a servant of the beard is among the most humble on this earth? You, however, are masters of the gun, infinite in justice and in generosity. If I can prove to you beyond doubt or objection that under the terms of his sentence Colonel Abu cannot possibly execute me, will you release me?'

The guards were flattered, curious and above all sceptical, so readily agreed.

'Then listen,' said the crafty Mehdi. 'It is the case that I must be executed on an unexpected day before the feast of Ramadan, which is now by my calculation no more than ten days away?'

'That is true,' said the guards.

'It is an incontrovertible fact that I must be executed within the following ten days, and also an incontrovertible fact that my execution must be unexpected?'

'It is Colonel Abu's pleasure,' said the guards.

'So,' continued Mehdi, 'I cannot be executed on the tenth day, on the eve of Ramadan, since, if I had not by then already been executed, that remaining day would be the only one on which I *could* be executed, and the execution would no longer be unexpected. Similarly, I cannot be executed on the ninth day, because with the tenth and final day eliminated, the ninth day would have become the final day, and the same arguments would apply. It is true also of the eighth day, and of the seventh, sixth, fifth, fourth, third and second days. It is true also of tomorrow. Either the whimsical Colonel Abu executes me unexpectedly or he does not execute me at all. Do you not agree?'

The guards looked at each other in wonderment. They were compelled to agree. After they had released him, Mehdi waved up at them from the dusty road outside the prison.

'Goodbye, my friends,' he shouted. 'You may freely visit my humble establishment at no cost to yourselves and I shall be as glad to see you there as I was unhappy to know you here, for did not Allah also say that the razor is no blunter than the human mind?'

And he walked away, still humming, 'Feed me with figs and I am yours for ever.'

The Love Knot

Three weeks after the amnesty, Ibn al Faid judged that it might be safe enough to return to his village. His family seemed so amazed at his suit and little attaché case that he believed they must have forgiven him for leaving at a time of danger. In fact they were amazed that he had dared to come back at all, and had no thought of forgiving him. However, they accepted his presents, and his mother and sister made a special dinner. It was what families must do.

After they had broken bread, Ibn summoned up enough courage to ask what had happened to his twin brother. Had he married Leila and left home? It was a tender topic, for Ibn himself had been known to favour the almond-eyed Leila before the troubles, and as the elder brother, if only by minutes, he had forbidden Hassan to pay court to her.

Alas, alas, they told him, Hassan had joined the rebels out of a foolish desire for personal success. He had been a hopeless rebel and had been caught at the earliest opportunity, trying to siphon petrol from Colonel Abu's land-rover. He was now in one of the prison camps that Colonel Abu had set up, and only the amnesty prevented him from being summarily executed.

That evening Leila and her father came to marvel at Ibn's success. She seemed as beautiful as ever, and when she stroked his pigskin attaché case with one tentative carmine fingernail, Ibn felt a shiver down his back as though he stood on a high turret. As the desire stirred in him, he didn't care what she might think of his desertion. He had to have her! How could he redeem himself in her eyes?

Ibn's feelings were perfectly evident to all of them, and they were amused to see that he had no idea about theirs. But he had always been like that: the world existed to give him the first suck at the breast, the last sweetmeat, the prettiest girl in the village, a pigskin briefcase. And he took no notice of anyone's feelings. Between them they worked out a daring scheme for Ibn to redeem himself, finely calculated so that even he could not refuse. Since visits were allowed, and since the authorities had no means of knowing that Hassan had a twin brother, it would be an easy matter for Ibn to go to the camp and switch clothes. Ibn was uneasy, but Leila fed him dates at each objection.

'They will see that we are twins when I arrive,' he said.

'Go in disguise,' said Leila. 'Go as a woman.'

'How can we change clothes?' asked Ibn.

'There are few guards,' said Leila. 'His friends will create a diversion.'

'How will I get out?' asked Ibn. 'They will think I am Hassan and keep me there.'

'That is a crucial point,' said Leila. 'You must have a distinguishing mark.'

'I have no distinguishing mark,' said Ibn. 'Brains are unfortunately not visible.'

'Then you must acquire one,' said Leila. 'We will take you to the tattooist, who will prick a love knot on to your chest. Look, like this one.' And she showed him her bosom. She blushed.

At this Ibn's doubts were cast aside. Little did he know that Leila did not blush for love of him, or for modesty, but because she thought him such a conceited idiot. She loved Hassan. She took him to the tattooist, who had been bribed to say nothing, and on the appointed day the heavily disguised Ibn visited Colonel Abu's prison camp. The flies and the stench disgusted him. He was brusque with his brother. He only wanted the whole thing to be over as soon as possible. He was astonished at how easy the exchange was, and waited impatiently until the agreed moment when Hassan would be safely back in the village.

Then he went to the guards and said: 'I am not Hassan al Faid. There has been a mistake. I am Ibn al Faid, a successful business man. You will have to release me.'

The guards laughed at him.

'You'd be amazed at the lengths the prisoners go to to try to get out of here,' they said. 'You'll have to do better than that. You look just like Hassan al Faid anyway, according to our records.'

'Of course I do,' said Ibn. 'But you see I have a distinguishing mark. It's my fiancée's love knot, woven on my chest in an endless expression of her love for me. And of mine for her, of course.'

And he thought of Leila popping dates into his mouth as he bared his chest before the guards, looking for anything like a desperado daring them to shoot him. Which they might well have done if there had been no amnesty, for the tattoo was no love knot. It was the secret mark of the rebels. There was hardly a prisoner in the whole camp who did not have one.

The guards only laughed the more. The amnesty wouldn't last for ever.

Symbols

The barber Mehdi was standing on a chair trying to bang a nail into the wall. Two out of three times he missed, and it was not long before he hit his thumb. He knew from cartoons in the newspaper what to do next: you must drop the hammer, clutch the thumb dramatically, or better still put it in your mouth, and utter words so unspeakably blasphemous that they can only be represented by meaningless typographical symbols chosen at whim by the cartoonist. Mehdi did all this, but he did not substitute the symbols.

His shop was in the oldest part of the city, where the spice-merchants and carpet-sellers plied their wares from what were little more than caves in the rocks upon which the city had been built, and therefore his walls were rough white-washed stone. After he had hit his hand a few more times, and bent a whole bag of nails, his first customer who happened to be a police spy, said: 'Why don't you give up, Mehdi? If you've taken such a dislike to your hand, you could make a full confession to the tax inspector and he'll have it off in no time! I'm getting tired of waiting.'

'Be patient, be patient,' said Mehdi. 'You're too early, anyway. I'm not open yet.'

And he cleared an upper shelf of the bottles of lotion that had been there for as long as anyone could remember and replaced them with the large portrait of Colonel Abu that he had been trying to hang on the wall. Then he got down to business.

The customer eyed the portrait suspiciously from beneath his steaming towels. Was all this for his benefit?

'I didn't think you were superstitious, Mehdi,' he said. 'Do you really believe that face will protect you? Everyone knows that you are a rebel at heart.'

'Me, a rebel?' protested Mehdi, whipping off the towels. 'I'm nothing of the sort. It's a well-established fact that a barber is quite outside politics, like a mullah. Everyone consults him on the most intimate and delicate matters. A customer beneath his towels is like a freshly blooming lily, open in all its innocence to Allah. The barber is a guardian of the spirit and must pay no attention to material things.'

He winked as he whipped up his fragrant foam in a little wooden bowl, and his customer roared with laughter.

'You're a cunning fellow, Mehdi,' he said. 'And you know how to save your own skin. Now be careful of my moustache.'

'True enough,' he replied. 'And a barber always has

to shave his own skin, too. Who else is there to do it for him?'

His customer nodded sagely at this.

'You see,' went on Mehdi, as his razor made its papery path through foam and bristle, 'the barber is wise because he is independent and he is independent because he is free. The leader of a country is nothing more, in effect, than an instrument in the hands of his people. He is an instrument of the popular will, a razor if you like. Or a hammer. The popular will decrees that some ancient practice is no longer tolerable. Strop, strop. It is swept away. Or a new law is required, to correct an injustice. With one blow it is enshrined in our constitution. But the leader is only the instrument by which these things are effected. The force behind him is that of the people. I speak now of symbols, for as all the true worshippers of Allah know, his world is made up out of symbols.

'You are not free, my friend, because you have yielded up your will to mine. You cannot shave yourself but must have it done for you. So it is with our people. They have yielded up their will to Colonel Abu, who is like razor and hammer combined. Our whole country is like a bruised thumb! Our beloved nation with a slit throat!'

The spy made some indeterminate noise as Mehdi pinched back his nose and the razor inched gently towards the boastful contours of his moustache.

'Talking of symbols,' said Mehdi, 'just as that pile

of bent nails shows that hanging is too good for Colonel Abu, the sharpness of this razor will reveal a police spy hoist with his own petard.'

And Mehdi shaved off the man's moustache.

Curfew

After he had put down the insurrection, Colonel Abu sent the army into the capital and announced a curfew. By that time the army was a poor thing on the whole, because only a few years earlier it had fought a full-scale war against the Colonel's foreign enemies. Its equipment and its traditions had taken a beating.

None the less, the Colonel surrounded the city with tanks and put one of the largest in the central square. It wasn't at all clear what it was intended to accomplish, since far from feeling cowed or shamed the people hurrying to work under its shadow were strangely elated. It made the humblest dishwasher or bootblack feel important, as though this evident emergency were due entirely to their own political volatility. Everyone rather enjoyed the sense of danger. No one noticed that the tank's gun barrel was badly dented and couldn't have fired a shell if it had wanted to.

Bakbak was a small government official who lived with his young wife in a privileged apartment block not far from the centre. They were not happy. Bakbak was an ardent but ineffective husband, and it had not been long before his wife had begun to mock him. Quite apart from finding this embarrassing and unseemly, he suspected that it was entirely due to her having known other men before she had married him. He couldn't prove it. He didn't even want to talk about it. She became cold and indifferent to him, and he learned to accept it.

Young soldiers were posted on duty at the entrances of all large buildings in the centre of the city. They were supposed to keep a tally of their building's occupants and to enforce the curfew, but in practice that was impossible. The soldiers were content to try simply to look important, though most of them were edgy and nervous at having to stand in a lobby all day long with small-arms at the ready.

The soldier on duty outside Bakbak's apartment building was quite as young as any of them. At first Bakbak pretended to take no notice of him. He told himself that he didn't care a jot about such surveillance. In reality he was terrified. Suppose the soldier took against him in some way, out of boredom or pure malice? His neighbours, many of whom were old and who stayed at home all day, could tell stories about him. He knew he was not popular. What happened once he had gone off to work? The guard was probably invited upstairs for some illicit drinking and primed with all sorts of gossip and complaint.

But once Bakbak had dared to have a good look at

him, he could see how young the guard was. A mere boy, with the bloom of youth upon him! Unlike all civilian men in the city he was clean shaven, and stood uncertainly in the doorway fingering his sten gun compulsively. Bakbak noticed how the boy's thumb kept brushing the oiled bolt of the weapon. It was the kind of gesture you saw on street corners and in the cafés where the lewd young men congregated, absently stroking the front of their trousers or even, as if no one could observe them, briefly cupping and lifting their contents, as if the very weight was momentarily uncomfortable, as if some ideal disposition had to be maintained, some mild constraint relieved.

Ah yes, he would be taken in, that young soldier, once he was familiar with the occupants! He would unhitch his obscene weapon on to the back of a chair and be grateful for the offered coffee. He would relax, make jokes, take greater freedoms. He was anyone's son or younger brother, anyone's young husband.

Bakbak was soon obsessed by the thought of the soldier in the apartment block after he had gone to work. He was free, wasn't he, to mount the stairs? To knock on doors? To rap with the butt of his gun on any door on any pretext?

Bakbak shuddered. And to think that the boy's only official purpose was to enforce the curfew! That is to say, to keep potentially violent men off the streets and away from each other. To keep them at home with their wives. To promote peace and the civic virtues on their foundation of marital accord.

Bakbak considered that to be a double obscenity. For what was marital accord, after all? Was it not, equally with politics, a matter of power? In his heart Bakbak was deeply shamed, for he knew he had no power. When one night his wife happened to make some gesture of appeasement, a tender yet unaccustomed motion of physical love, the shock, regret, shame and self-disgust in Bakbak's soul fused into blind anger like a mathematical equation, cold and inevitable. What else could have promoted such desire in his wife? He went out in his rage and tears and did what he thought any righteous Colonel Abu would have done. He seized the young soldier's gun and smashed his face with it, repeatedly, against the concrete pillars of the building.

Then he sat down in the road and awaited the consequences.

Loyalty

I am Colonel Abu's physician. You would think that I am in the perfect position to put him out of the way. I am probably envied for the glory and gratitude I could bring upon myself by getting rid of the hated dictator. But I cannot do it. It is no humanitarian weakness, rather a matter of trust. It is quite simple to explain.

Before I was promoted, I was the chief consultant at the city hospital. I had received my training in France, so always felt something of an outsider. One's professional competence is an invisible commodity and therefore a free passport to success, but my wife was from Lyon. I was called on to treat the Colonel now and again, for there were times when Dr al Ma'aruf was not available, or temporarily out of favour, but I got the impression that I was an object of suspicion.

'You are a colonial relic, of course,' Dr al Ma'aruf had once said to me, filling up my glass with the revolting peach nectar that was *de rigeur* at parties in government circles. 'The Colonel must think of you as having a secret cellar of burgundy and cognac.'

Since that was precisely what I did have, I could only smile ruefully.

'Better than a cellar full of grenades,' I said.

'Allah is forgiving,' said Dr al Ma'aruf.

I quite liked the old fellow, but I couldn't always tell what he was thinking. It was as though Colonel Abu's own paranoia were infectious. In any absolute government there is little sense of hierarchy at the top. You can't expect much support. Or no more, at least, than the loyalty you are prepared to give yourself. And that is no guarantee of anything at all. The reality is that everyone is prepared to stab everyone else in the back.

So it was that when Dr al Ma'aruf telephoned me in the middle of the night asking me to be prepared to confirm a false diagnosis of diabetes in our beloved leader, I did not know what to think.

'I would have set this up more carefully long ago,' he said, his voice cracking with emotion. 'But my own life is in danger. My plan has to be virtually extemporised, you see. And now I desperately need your help.'

The proposal was simply to provide early and frequent opportunity to inject Colonel Abu with the five to ten millimetres of air (instead of insulin) that might give him an undetectable embolism. Dr al Ma'aruf had made his 'diagnosis'. The sceptical Colonel Abu had naturally proposed to consult me for a second opinion. If we presented a united front, then the Colonel might be quickly dispatched.

Were assassinations really as simple as this, I wondered? Was Dr al Ma'aruf as simple? Did he not consider that all our telephones might be tapped? Why had he decided to confide in me in the first place (or perhaps it was the second place)? I might have been someone wholly faithful to the Colonel, ready to betray the conspiracy immediately. What a risk he would be taking!

In fact I was as eager to be rid of the Colonel as anyone, for private as well as public reasons. Yet I made only equivocal remarks over the telephone. Not only might the telephone system be bugged, but, as soon came to me with dismaying force, Dr al Ma'aruf himself might be simply testing my loyalty to the regime. He would be doing so on Colonel Abu's behalf, naturally, possibly with a promotion in view. If my career were to be advanced in any way it would, I could quite see, be necessary to know whether my cognac might in practice be extended to grenades.

I was in a quandary. What a political opportunity this was! What a dangerous move to make! I tried to calculate the chances. In the end I did nothing, and within the week Dr al Ma'aruf 'disappeared'.

Now that I have inherited his job you will see why I dare not risk a similar plot.

The Switch

Ibrahim put his hand out to the switch, as instructed. He was conscious only of his forefinger reaching for it, almost touching it. He had all the time in the world. But were these his instructions? Had he really been so instructed? He could not remember.

And why should he be complying with orders? He did not know that either. There didn't seem to be anything much in his head except for his consciousness of the switch. He felt very tired, as though he had been on a long journey.

He had to press the switch!

But did he really have to? He hadn't pressed it yet, and nothing terrible had happened. Perhaps the intention, or the appearance of intention, was enough. Perhaps if he did press it something terrible would happen. He searched his head for something other than the image of the switch, something that might begin to explain to him what he was really doing. What was his name, for example?

He couldn't think of his name!

For a second or two he tried to be constructive about

his ignorance. 'Surely,' he said to himself, 'surely if I cannot remember my own name I must not press this switch?' And he asked himself who he could be who was worth reducing to this state of abject duty.

Suddenly it dawned on him that he was not the barber Mehdi, for he could hear Mehdi's voice somewhere in the very back of his head telling him that he mustn't get caught. Mustn't get caught doing what? Mustn't get caught pressing the switch perhaps? No, that didn't seem quite right. He had the feeling that he had already been caught, and the voice of Mehdi was not only warning him but reproving him. No, he was not Mehdi, because Mehdi was someone who didn't so easily get caught. Mehdi made it his business to enrage Colonel Abu, but always managed to twist out of his grasp.

Colonel Abu. That was somebody else, then, that he wasn't. But though he wasn't Colonel Abu, it might be Colonel Abu who was making him press the switch when he clearly didn't know why he was pressing it. If he could discover why, he could choose.

His finger was touching the switch, and in a moment he had passed from having all the time in the world to having no time at all. Even in that passing moment he was aware that the switch was not a common switch; not, for example, the pert brass salute of his old bedside lamp, nor the rocking plastic cradle of the light switch in his office.

This enlightenment came too late. All at once,

knowing that he worked in an office, he knew what that work was, and for what he was now wanted. He reviewed all the switches that he had ever felt beneath his finger, and knew that the one meeting his finger was the wrong one. He knew that the consequences of pressing it were unknown and dangerous. His memory now reminded him of pain, which was therefore inevitably associated with the switch, like an equation. Pain equalled switch. Switch equalled pain. He had been instructed in pain. He was being tested. Why couldn't someone else press the switch? Why couldn't Colonel Abu, if it were he indeed, press the switch?

I am Ibrahim, he suddenly remembered. I have been put to some extreme, the result of my own willing course of action. If I do not want to press the switch, nothing worse can happen to me than would happen if I press it. I can still be a hero.

But he pressed the switch.

Colonel Abu's Question

When Colonel Abu made such fools of the English and French Ambassadors, half the world was delighted. The other half was appalled. But that was only to be expected. That was the political reality, and no one could remember when the affairs of the Middle East had been any different.

But what was not expected was the way in which it was done. A paradox like that, almost a kind of teasing, wasn't Colonel Abu's style at all. He was capable of suspense, certainly. He was unpredictable. And he was downright cruel. But this, why this was almost witty! Someone else had to be behind it.

Of course, it was the barber Mehdi.

Mehdi was always in trouble with Colonel Abu's regime, even though he used to claim, raising his upturned palms as if to bear the weight of his great innocence, that barbers were above politics. The Colonel's military police knew otherwise, and whenever they came to arrest him would shake their heads in despairing affection.

'You know everything that's going on, Mehdi,' they said. 'So how can you possibly be innocent?'

'It's true that I know everything,' nodded Mehdi. 'It is my gift from Allah, and I must suffer the consequences with patience.'

After his latest arrest, Mehdi was confined with some foreign hostages in relatively comfortable conditions in the old printing works in the city itself. The guards even offered him the occasional cigarette. They said that since the cessation of the amnesty all the gaols and camps were quite full.

'How can that be?' thought Mehdi. 'They have put me here for some reason. They must want me to spy on these foreign journalists. They imagine that since a barber knows everything I will be approached by these journalists and rapidly be befriended by them as a source of information. Then they will want me to obtain information myself. And then we will all be shot together. I must find a way out of this one.'

After much wheedling and bribing of guards and other officials, Mehdi obtained an audience with Colonel Abu himself. When he was alone with Colonel Abu, he smiled ingratiatingly as only a true servant of the beard can.

'Colonel,' he fawned, bowing low so that his forehead almost touched the Colonel's shining boots. 'Excellency. Everyone knows the justice of your cause, and of your own justice. Justice itself in Allah's eyes is freshly defined by your very existence, which has been such a gift to our people.'

'Get to the point,' growled Colonel Abu.

'We know, do we not, my Colonel,' said Mehdi, 'how foolish and hypocritical these Western politicians are? They uphold the doubtful principle of freedom, and yet will not pay the ransom to release any of their spies and liars that you have apprehended at their dirty work and kept confined at the Sul'addin Printing Works.'

Colonel Abu had never actually thought of asking for a ransom, and wondered how many British tanks a newspaper journalist might be worth.

'And to keep these journalists in a derelict printing works!' continued Mehdi. 'Excellency, that was a stroke of genius. For did not Allah say that the life of a nation lies in symbols?'

Colonel Abu nodded. He was listening now.

'Excellency, I have a proposal,' said Mehdi. 'I will not conceal from you my deep desire for my own liberty. Doubtful a principle as we agree it to be, I do have a beautiful wife who is faint for want of my devotions, and walking the streets of the city are honest men growing unnaturally hairy in my absence. All I ask from you is that you give me a chance of freedom by posing three questions.'

'I have to ask three questions?' asked a puzzled Colonel Abu.

'Not of me, I hasten to add,' said Mehdi. 'But of

my wife. And of the British Ambassador. And the French Ambassador. And because these questions, apparently trivial as they will be, are bound to have significant political consequences, I suggest that they be conducted in public, with full media attention.'

Thus it was that on the following day began and ended the briefest negotiation about hostages that the world has ever known. So brief was it indeed, that when the most popular radio programme was interrupted to carry it live to the nation, the same song was still playing when it had finished as was playing when it had begun, and what is more the song happened to be Mehdi's favourite: 'Feed me with figs and I am yours for ever.'

The hostages in question were plump Julian Naseby of the *Observer*, Ado Willy of *Paris Soir*, and Mehdi himself – all men of little political importance who had now reached their finest, or perhaps one should say most ignominious, hour. For fame, even on the absurdist terms in which she now offered herself, is a great distiller of personality and circumstance, and for a time, as Mehdi was well aware, a man can become a symbol.

To the English Ambassador, and to the French Ambassador, and to Mehdi's wife, all of whom were 'on the line', as though partaking in some trivial quiz-show, Colonel Abu asked the same question. What is more, he appeared in person to do so, as he did in times of public crisis or public triumph. The nation hung on his words, and the foreign stations also hovered, like spectators at a street accident.

'You have five seconds,' said Colonel Abu. 'I want an immediate answer. My enemies accuse me of never keeping my word, but I promise on the future of our nation that I shall do so. The hostages shall either be released or shot. I shall release each hostage if you can correctly answer my question. And the question which I now put to you is: "Am I lying if I say that I will shoot your hostage?" '

The consternation in each embassy may be imagined. The English Ambassador, a man of bluff charm destined for the lodgings of an Oxbridge College, thought for a second and said 'Yes,' because he could not believe that if Abu was promising to release Naseby he could also be about to shoot him. The French Ambassador was a more devious type altogether, usually managing to keep two mistresses at once, (currently in Nice and Ajaccio). He allowed himself a full four seconds before also saying 'Yes,' on the grounds that Abu was indeed an inveterate liar. Both men dimly perceived behind the double negatives the possibility that if they predicted release, and Abu did release the men, then they would indeed have predicted correctly.

Both Naseby and Willy were immediately shot, thus confounding the Ambassador's predictions and therefore allowing Abu's action.

Mehdi's wife, however, unhesitatingly replied 'No,'

thus confounding Colonel Abu, for if (as she was predicting) he was not lying when he proposed to shoot her husband, then he would indeed shoot him, and her answer to his question would have been correct. But according to Abu's promise (witnessed by millions over the air) this correct answer was bound to secure Mehdi's release.

Mehdi had not explained this part of the game to Colonel Abu, and it left the Colonel in an impotent rage, like the donkey between two bales of hay. Mehdi had however explained it carefully to his wife. He had once thought it a very wise provision against future arrest. And he was right.

V

THE BORED GOD

The Void

Here I am on this ledge, quite unable to get down. Is it a ledge or a lip, a sort of worn sand-hole miles above nothing? It resembles, maybe, the rim of an eye shrunk in its socket to an absence. If it really is such a thing, then I am clinging to a giant statue. Suppose I were dreaming it, then it might have been suggested by Cary Grant's exploits in the last minute of *North by Northwest* where he is climbing down a presidential visage on Mount Rushmore. But since I am *not* dreaming it, and it is evidently real, then the fact that the analogy occurs to me must mean that I'm not in immediate danger.

Why is this? My situation is extreme. I've no means of descending by whatever route I came. Is it that I picture my predicament so fancifully as a way of postponing the moment when I must effect a rescue? Of, as it were, aesthetically nerving myself to accept the fact of being so stuck? Perhaps this self-consciousness is the only way to accept the reality, which otherwise would be too terrible to contemplate, since I can half-pretend that none of it is serious; that I could after all, if I wish it, reach for some tiny escape-hole, previously unnoticed, small as a tear-duct; that wooden towers of ineffable complication could be wheeled up beside me, swaying with their immense height, perhaps not able to come close enough to be grasped. But the very unlikeliness of these modes of rescue tells me that the situation is serious after all.

At the moment of realising this I now see that there *is* a way down, a cavity outside, beyond and to one side of, the narrow crevice on which I've found my temporary refuge. I see faces within it, looking out at me. They are like the faces of the tourists who have climbed a great tower and are slightly fearful of squeezing through on to the roof. At the same time their expressions are of practical concern for me and my predicament. Without anxiety they are making preparations to receive me. They can't think how I can have got stuck out here. I should not be here, because it isn't safe.

But how much less safe to reach out and join them! There is nothing firm to hold on to, and no certainty of being assisted. I should have to leave my ledge irrevocably in order to make any attempt on that hole. There would be a sickening moment of unbalance before I could be sure of getting a grasp. I couldn't count on having the strength to pull myself in even then. I must lunge outwards and upwards, over the void.

Those faces may disappear. They may be the only

chance I have. To settle back, as if for resigned contemplation of my fate or of the distant war that is the half-forgotten context of my isolation, is to issue a challenge to them. I am saying that I require a more organised rescue. I'm not prepared to take the risk. How is this to be done, if indeed I do it? Do I huddle pathetically, simply waiting for strong arms, ropes, a system of pulleys? Do I take out binoculars with insouciance, expecting them to be horrified? Can I count on their concern to be put to any practical use at all? I don't have any right to behave like this. I didn't have any choice.

I know that I must tackle the void, but just for now, to pretend that I'm utterly incapable of doing so is the greatest pleasure in the world.

The Vision

I was doing something totally insignificant when I had my vision, something hardly worth remembering at all. Still, I'll give you an idea of the circumstances. I was in the Polo, waiting to turn into the Summertown car park. The Banbury Road traffic is nearly always steady enough to make a wait necessary, but luckily there are crossing lights, and it's never long before somebody punches the button. I do recollect thinking that the whole trip was quite unnecessary because I was only going to my bank with some business that really ought to have been possible by phone.

There I was, my hands on the steering-wheel, waiting to turn. It was the middle of the day and quite busy. It was drizzling slightly. My glasses-case, bank deposit book and shopping-list were on the seat beside me. I was tapping the wheel with one finger, and turning over in my head that confused assortment of routine hopes and intentions usually to be found there, when suddenly I had this vision.

I should make it clear that I am someone quite without religious belief or observance. In fact I suppose I take an unusually absolute position, having, for example, been a Fellow of an Oxford college for twenty-five years without once having attended a service in its chapel, despite the renown of its choir. Tempting providence, some might say. Ripe for a humiliating revelation.

But the vision didn't seem to me to reveal anything, and I certainly didn't feel humble. Deeply surprised, of course, and interested. Absorbed, I suppose you'd say. Too absorbed to be shocked at first, at least while it was happening. I wasn't conscious of time passing, but then one often isn't in cases of sudden perception. For instance, a moment earlier I'd noticed a woman dodging the traffic with a plant she'd obviously just bought from the nursery. I had time to notice a great deal about her, knitted red hat, heavy glasses, tweed skirt whose length seemed to indicate quite precisely both her social class and intelligence, feathery characteristics of the plant, almost a sapling in fact, and so on. If required I could have written pages about her and I don't suppose my eyes were on her for more than two and a half seconds.

Now because of this ability to see so quickly, and because of my understandable absorption in my vision, surprising as it was, I have simply no idea how long it lasted. Looking back on it, and trying to be as accurate as possible (remembering, for example, whether there were many pedestrians at the lights and judging how long they might have been waiting for them to change), I would say that it could hardly have lasted for more than about five seconds.

Hardly a vision, more like a glimpse! The trouble is (and this is where you're going to be disappointed) I can't describe it at all. I can hardly even tell you where it was. It wasn't exactly in the car, and certainly wasn't outside it. It was sort of instead of the car, or part of it. It was something like a patch, but on both sides of me at once. I didn't lose sight of the road or the lights, and part of me knew when to make my turn and was ready to do so. But there was this patch, this partial presence or busy absence at some significant vantage point in relation to myself. What it was, what it actually consisted of, I'm afraid I simply can't translate into ordinary terms of shape, motion, colour, and so on. I didn't feel I was seeing it with my senses at all.

And of course the strangest thing about it was that I didn't feel that it was me seeing it, but quite the reverse. Although this busy patch was (how shall I put it?) behaving in some way, unfolding if you like, I got the impression that it was observing me. You could say that I didn't have my vision at all. My vision had *me*.

It wasn't beatific or anything. I've read some of the mystics and recognise nothing in what they write. Of course, they knew what they were looking for, and they had a religious language with which to look at it. And language is in any case performative. It creates drama. In linguistic terms, we need the language to make sense of the experience, just as syntax transforms into some comprehensible embodiment the deep structure of our concepts. What was so unnerving about the vision was not so much that I could summon no language or syntax with which to embody it, but that its deep structure had no semantic value for me. Not only was it incommunicable, it was beyond my conceptual power as well.

Inconceivable, you will say. Perhaps. But of value? Possibly. I couldn't estimate its value or do anything with it, as I could with my bank deposit. But its unique otherness, its untranslatable existence, its simply having happened, seemed then and still seems (however banal its subsequent status as an experience) the most important thing that has ever happened to me.

The Gypsy Singer

I had told myself that I wouldn't eat another cherry until four o'clock. It was 3.40. I went into the kitchen to look at the clock that is provided as part of the oven timing-mechanism. It indicated 10.55. So I ate another cherry in the kitchen and said that I wouldn't eat another until midday.

Back in the sitting room I put the gypsy singer on the record-player and took out a pad of writing paper.

'I don't write fan letters,' I began, but crossed it out because it seemed a paradoxical way to begin a fan letter. It also seemed a bit self-centred, even self-satisfied. As though there were a particular virtue in not writing fan letters, when big stars like the gypsy singer got them all the time. What would she think?

Having thought for a while about what she might think I decided that anyone as beautiful and talented as the gypsy singer wouldn't actually like getting fan letters all the time. They'd be boring after a while. I began again.

'I'm sure you don't like getting fan letters all the time,' I wrote. 'But don't worry, because I don't know how to find out your address, so I won't be able to send this one.'

This was paradoxical too, so I tore it up, and just listened to the record.

The music was a strange affair: hand-drums, strings, a droning instrument like a bagpipe, something else that kept up a rattle. It repeated itself endlessly, propelling itself onward like a camel train lurching across the dunes. Her voice wove a complaint around it as though she were swaying in a basketwork cage in the midst of it, being carried off against her will. This complaint was forced out of her and yet seemed to give her extreme pleasure, for the warbled phrases all descended at last to a small voiced gasp as though she were exultant at having conquered her disgust enough to put a small damp squirming lizard out of the window. The driven melody was therefore punctuated as if by cries of love. The caravan had nowhere particular to get to, but it was making a good deal out of the process.

That's it, I reflected. That's all it is. Nowhere in mind, but just the getting there. Like spacing out the cherries. The record ended.

By this time it was 4.04. Four minutes without a cherry! I was doing myself a disservice, so I ate two. I immediately felt guilty, and decided that one of them would have to count as my next kitchen cherry, even though there was at least forty minutes to go before I was allowed to eat it. At that rate I would run out of cherries before the day was over. And I didn't even know which clock was right. I was living by two different time-scales, like living with two different lives. How long could I keep that up?

I imagined being two quite different people, as different as my own whim allowed me to be. One of them would be utterly reliable, never breaking rules, never anticipating cherries. The other could be anything at all, a guzzler, a rude letter-writer, an exhibitionist. He could look out of the kitchen window for passing girls and do terrible things in their sight while pretending not to have seen them.

I felt almost excited by this, and went into the kitchen as though entering the forbidden quarter of a city. The cooker clock still said 10.55.

It's bloody stopped, I said. So I went back into the sitting room and put on the other side of the gypsy singer.

Alternative Reality

It's in the very nature of desire to be about nothing but itself. You can prove that at the most basic level, linguistically. Take any of those equally vague words that attempt to describe the objects of our desire, such as fame, pleasure, God, and so on. You can feel them making an effort to attach themselves to something palpable. You'd agree that this mere effort, pathetic as its outcome might be, at least demonstrates a trust in the possibility of palpability, or shall we say the identifiable. They are nouns, aren't they? Distinguished the one from the other by this very identity-function, however imprecise it may be in practice. But desire itself doesn't distinguish. It's perhaps the strongest of all the acting or willing states that give their energy to the language in the form of verbs. Verbs, the keystones of syntax! Without which the whole linguistic edifice would come tumbling down. Desire is the supreme unattached predicate, symbol of our condition of uncompleteness.

For this reason it can hardly ever matter that we don't really know what it is that we desire. The desiring is everything. We can desire the most ridiculous things.

Take that thing in the computer. Well, not in the computer itself. It was in a computer game, a piece of software, and so must have been created by the person who wrote the program. But it was very strange. There was nothing at all about it in the description of the game. You'd have thought it would have said somewhere that you might find it. Or were even expected to look for it, as part of the game. It must have used quite a lot of memory.

You'll know the sort of game I mean. It was one of those that simulates flight. The computer screen becomes the window of a cock-pit through which one can see the features of a landscape which the computer program creates for you as you move around in it by manipulating various keys. It is nothing more than a mechanical illusion, but while you are playing the game the illusion works. The landscape is somehow really there 'in' the computer, and although for reasons of economy of memory it is remarkably simplified (mine was created entirely from white lines on black, giving the impression of flying by night), while the machine is running you believe in its existence. After all it notionally extends to five or six square miles. It contains mountains, a river with a bridge across it, and a distant city, consisting of three or four ghostly tower blocks, like a cartoon of a Western desert town. You can climb to fifty thousand feet, and you attempt to fly under the bridge. You can land and take off again if the ground is flat enough. And when you have found the city itself, which is not always easy to find, you can fly between the buildings of the city if you tilt the plane on its side.

Childish stuff, you will say. But like language itself it is an alternative reality, and no doubt a model, in its way, of our deepest wishes. Perhaps no one played it as much as I did. Perhaps for some reason I was less easily bored.

At any rate, in the middle of one rainy afternoon I suddenly found myself not flying dangerously on one wing tip through the deserted city but somehow having managed to land the plane just outside it. I had often crashed into the city or flown over it. I had landed elsewhere in the landscape. But I had never been stationary so near the city before. What in flight was always a looming adjustment of crude and glimmering lines on my screen, drawing and re-drawing the perspective in that not-quite-instantaneous way that computer programs have, was in stillness a façade of perfect cubes, as though made of black glass against a black sky, empty as office-blocks at 3 a.m. Since I was no longer using 'energy' I could have stayed there for ever, mesmerised by my unaccustomed proximity to the motionless city. I could see down the mainstreet, at the end of which something moved.

My astonishment at this was, as you might understand, modified by the normal reactions of the player of computer games. I felt that there must be a couple of new keys on the keyboard with which I could control or respond to whatever it was that had flitted across my vision. There it was again! I could hardly say what it was, except that it was quite unlike the ordinary visual display of the game. That is to say that as far as I could see it was solid, and coloured. It was detailed and animated too, except that I didn't have time to focus on the details. It seemed a bit like something that in another sort of game you would have to fire at, but I didn't want to fire at it. What was it like? Before I could see, it had disappeared again. But I had the impression of a sort of involuted peacock, a kind of snakeskin turnip swallowing and renewing its skin, an elusive thing, partly innocent, partly mischievous. I tried to taxi round the city to find it, but must have bumped over an electronic boulder and crumpled an imaginary wing-tip. I had to abort the game, and haven't succeeded in sighting the creature since. I even wrote to the publishers of the game, but I didn't get a reply. They must have thought me as crazy as you do.

As I said, we can desire the most ridiculous things. Even things that we know are not real. For in the end the purest form of desire is precisely that thing which can never be fulfilled. The things we need are the things that their wanting calls into being, a mechanistic form of desire concerned with simply perpetuating ourselves: sleep, food, sex. Real desire is for the unknown, that trick of language called the intransitive. My creature lurking in its invented landscape was a trick like that, a trick such as a lexicographer might play, or a bored writer of computer programs, or a bored god.

Machines

It must have been the knocking that awakened me, even though it had featured in the dream I woke from. And that of course is the way with the futile nightly holiday of the brain, cramming in its trivial souvenirs and trophies right up to the last moment when it makes that last-minute dash for the train to reality.

Is it really like that for the brain? Does it weary of its daily work of laborious rationalising and long for periodic escape as a tourist of the contingent? Does it crave an expansiveness and well-being denied by the routines of causality and logic?

I doubt it. These freedoms are often very far from relaxing. Dreams are full of terror. And they can be such bloody hard *work*. You can wake from them with a great sense of relief that the morning is going to bring nothing more taxing than the making of toast, the running of hot water, the filling of a fountain pen. That knocking, for example: it featured as a great performance in the sky, a disaster; slow machines with coloured parts, bits spinning off as they passed over. At the same time I knew that the noise was made by detonations in the quarry. All this could be accommodated into a scenario of delayed rescue and indulged anxiety.

But once I was awake I realised that they had stopped working the quarry years ago. Somebody at the door? I was at the bedroom window in a second, but could see nothing. I didn't really need to go downstairs to the front door to know that there was nobody there. There are fields all round the cottage, and a visitor, whether arriving or departing, is visible for hundreds of yards.

Still, reality had intruded. And, as is the paradoxical way with reality, it had proved less explicable than the expensive drama of my dream, and less involving.

As I actually did fill my pen and sat down to write this story I reflected that in our natural life, which we have long abandoned, there would have been terror in abundance. Nature thrives on pursuit and escape. We have civilised it out of existence and perhaps, in truth, we long to restore that daily knocking of the blood at the nearness of some predator, some primal fear that is a condition of our precarious existence. If so, then, the sleeping brain is upon a necessary adventure, allowing us to suffer, to hunt and be hunted. It is in the business of secreting adrenalin, accelerating the heart-beat, imagining long-lost muscles, as though fulfilling a determined motion.

I hadn't been writing for long, or no longer at any rate than the boiling of the second kettle of the morning, when the knocking began again. It sounded so much like someone at the door that in the act of starting up out of my chair I had already reviewed in my mind the likely identity of my visitor. But I immediately saw that it was no human visitor.

It was a blue jay at the window, pecking hungrily at the putty in the frame. It seemed enormous, perhaps half the height of the window, intent and muscular beneath its motley of grey, black and blue, straddled on the sill, the beak working. The putty was quite recent, I remembered, for the pane had been replaced. Of course, it was delicious to the bird. I remembered its seedy fragrance as I had kneaded the oily mass in my hand before thumbing it into the groove between the wood and the glass.

For some reason it didn't see me in the dimness behind the cottage curtains. I was able, therefore, with a strange concentration and primitive stealth to reach my arm through the open half of the window, inch by unobserved inch, slowly as a watched clock, and seize the bird in my hand, pinioning one struggling wing, my thumb just failing to reach the other so that it immediately extended and beat wildly like the released elastic of a toy propeller. It was only a moment, but it was like the whole of life packed in there beneath the warm feathers before I released it, the heart of a palpable hectic machine, battering in delight at its own danger.

Limbo

Were they arriving or departing, these people? Had they already been there, and were returning? Or were they only now, after long preparation, ready to go? Had they perhaps forgotten about their journey?

If explanations had been, as they hardly were, at all necessary, then this last might have been the most credible. How easy it was to forget! The few poor belongings once unpacked, could familiarise the meanest room. You didn't expect the authorities to provide even a table or a chair, knowing that small comforts could be taken as an inducement to stay. Any accommodation you were eventually lucky enough to find might even have had the nails removed from the walls, since a picture easily hung is an instant window into the past. The view through the real window might be an alien chaos of transit, haggling and dispossession, but the framed plover or estuary of your childhood bedroom will quickly habituate you to the strangeness of a lodging. And then another day there, and then another, is soon found bearable.

I met one of them, a girl, at the market. She had

been confused about the currency and had been about to pay far too much for some paltry withered root vegetables. She thanked me so eagerly that I felt it wouldn't be out of place to walk some way with her, perhaps even back to her tenement. She had a plain, rather doughy face and uneven teeth, but her eyes were beautiful.

'It's easy to feel that one doesn't belong,' I said, meaning to reassure her.

She looked puzzled.

'Look at me,' I went on. 'I'm an old hand, after all, and even I find it a difficult or dangerous place sometimes. That feeling of not belonging: you know, it's quite natural. It's just that the longer you get used to feeling it, the harder it is to think of returning. And that must be a good thing, don't you agree?'

She said nothing, but looked at me as if I were propounding some deep concepts of metaphysical philosophy.

I took her hand. Such an innocent! It was not, oddly enough, a hard-worked hand. It had a plumpness, and its knuckles were dimples. Someone, I could see, protected and loved her. Did that someone find it convenient to keep her in ignorance, too?

'From our perspective,' I continued, 'everything is marginalised, simply because everything leads to the margin. We're all outsiders here. And I happen to believe that we should help each other. To make things tolerable.'

I couldn't tell whether her big frightened eyes were silently seeking more explanations, starved of them as she clearly was, or whether they were conscious that already she was straying on her errand and might be learning too much for her own comfort. I lifted the plump little hand to my lips briefly before she ran away.

What a sadness to me, this fear of knowledge! After all, a margin should be a place of comment and analysis, a place indeed quite outside the remorseless ongoing authority of the text, a timeless place of stasis and perspective. It was their fear, wasn't it, that made of it such a hurt limbo? As though it were any sort of answer, to run away.

What was on the other side, their side? Was it like ours, a place from which the presently marginalised had presumably once arrived? Was it the place to which our own journey must be made? Why is it that we still have the journey in mind? Will we forget too? And what about returning? Since we never return, then the fact that they don't is immaterial. We, too, when all is said and done, claim that we can go back at any time we like.

Second Report on the Planet

I knew that there had to be an explanation of the phenomenon of 'death' about which I sent in an earlier report. As you rightly observed, such conditions of existence as I described must be insupportable. To travel uncertainly from one such extreme helplessness only to arrive ultimately at a state of even greater helplessness made all the more poignant for the heightened consciousness imparted by the experience on the way – this would surely lead to a mass rebellion of the individuals called by circumstances to make this terrible journey. I looked for signs of organised resistance to these conditions, but found none. It is true that a few of these inhabitants of the planet voluntarily abandon their journey, but these are looked upon as insane, and are generally viewed with awe. Even when envy of them is hypocritically expressed, it is notable that their example is not followed.

I felt that there must be some explanation of this general resignation, and began to look more closely at the origins of individuals. If their destiny was breakdown, destruction and oblivion, perhaps the secret of their persistence lay not in ends but in beginnings (and this time I was determined to avoid confusion of the two).

Where did these individuals come from? I had never observed the stage beyond helplessness. A natural tact and pity compelled me to turn away my attention, though I knew that such fastidiousness was unprofitable. I had to discover the truth!

There had to be a secret reason, not only for the extraordinary stoicism and forgetfulness about 'death' (given that at the same time it was much feared), but for the nature of the physical arrangements themselves, so wasteful of human effort in the perpetual re-learning of even the basic skills. We order things differently, as you know!

It didn't take very long to discover this secret. The answer is that each one comes out of another one! Each one, that is to say, was once, without exception, inside another one. And is then delivered up, in a state of incompletedness, into a general conspiracy to pretend that this state of incompletedness can ever be satisfactorily transcended. It is no wonder that life on this planet is so unsatisfactory. Think of it. There is not only the waste of wisdom I have described, but the arduous and unperfected method of acquiring it. Their individuals have actually to be created afresh, in a lengthy and uncertain process which causes much anxiety, only to face individual extinction and the intolerable burden of being perpetually distracted from the pursuit of knowledge by the need themselves to allow new individuals to come out of them. This process so absorbs all their energies that they have naturally become ashamed of it. This is why they have made it secret, as far as it is possible for them to do so.

How strange, then, that they have never noticed the logical connection between these two salient factors of their strange existence, the passage from helplessness to helplessness and the inevitable coming of each one out of another one. These innumerable little parabolas of experience which they call life (even, in their great naïvety, 'lives'), belong not to individuals at all. They are like the blown spores of a single organism, the replenished cells or repeated pulse of the true macro-individual. They are not a 'they' at all, but an 'it', as we should have known from the primitive form of their behaviour. It is their secret shame but also their secret compensation for 'death', since 'they' may die, but 'it' never does.

What are the origins of this 'it', you will enquire? If each one has come out of another one, the process must be traceable back to a beginning. The first one out of which another one came may well have contained in essence all the many imperfections of their organic system. I still do not admire the life of this planet, but I shall continue to investigate this particular problem and send in my reports.

VI

SECRETS

The Alpenorpheon

I was terribly excited by my latest find, and immediately took it along to Mr Paul, the chap at Graveney's who does my bassoon keys when they stick. It didn't have a case, of course, so I had to be very careful getting it in and out of the car, and one of the assistants had to hold open the door for me. It caused quite a stir in the front of the shop. A young clarinettist I knew slightly was buying some reeds and he immediately wanted to play it. I told him he wouldn't be able to get a sound out of it. I'd tried all day. Other customers crowded round.

Mr Paul rescued me, and took us into his inner sanctum at the back. He was, I must say, quite as excited as I was. He looked it up and down and stroked its great silver headpiece and said: 'Well, you've excelled yourself this time, haven't you?'

I was thrilled. I spent a good deal at Graveney's, both on my own bassoon's account, and on having the various instruments done up that I acquired for my collection. They were polite about my junk-shop fifes and did what they could with the cracks in old

143

church clarinets that I found. But they were not often impressed. When I said I'd found it in a place in Sevenoaks and paid less than they were charging for a fairly run-of-the-mill Welsh dresser, I could see that Mr Paul was more than a little envious.

'You can multiply that by fifty for a start,' he said. 'Mind you, it'll take some putting in order.'

'What is it?'

'I *think* it's called an "alporpheum",' said Mr Paul. 'It's extremely rare. I've certainly never handled one. The point is that it produces the deepest note of any musical instrument, two octaves below the pedal bass of the great organ in Cologne Cathedral.'

It did indeed look rather like a great organ pipe, with its multiple lengths of rich dark wood bound in hoops of silver and surmounted by its moulded silver headpiece with a frieze of grapes and bears. I had cleaned it, of course. I don't think the shop in Sevenoaks had looked at it very closely. They obviously had no idea what it was. And I very nearly hadn't bought it anyway, because Barbara had become more than visibly bored and had threatened to make a scene if we didn't get back in time for her rehearsal. (I got the feeling that lunch at Tiffin's was all she'd really come for, and that had been disappointing.)

When Mr Paul mentioned a figure for the cost of putting it in order I nearly had a fit. But he assured me it was worth it.

'Look,' he said. 'If I can get it into a playable condition you could sell it tomorrow and buy a house with the proceeds. Let me see what I can do, and I'll give you a ring.'

I felt encouraged by that. I'd sacrificed a lot to my collection, which took up most of one of my two rooms in Islington. It was time I settled down. I had a steady job in one of the BBC orchestras, and there was Barbara. Or was there Barbara? I was never quite sure, because she blew hot and cold. Or perhaps I should say sharp and flat. And things were a bit flat at the moment. That is to say, she wasn't in mine. Perhaps if I had a house things would be better? They would certainly be better if she showed any sort of enthusiasm for me personally. Physically, I mean.

'Do you mean a family house?' I asked Mr Paul hopefully.

'Possibly,' he said, with an amused look.

'In Islington?'

'More like Sevenoaks.'

In the months while I was waiting for the reconditioning of the alporpheum I must confess that I not only didn't get further with Barbara: things took a distinctly retrograde turn. For instance, one evening when I'd got her bra off I became somehow mesmerised by the red creases it had left on her ribs. None of the pictures of girls that I'd ever seen had those. It rather put me off, and of course Barbara was quick to notice. She's hardly a furnace of desire herself. I really needed *her* to become more interested in *me*.

'There we are,' said Mr Paul, when I called in again at Graveney's. 'New key-pads and springs, three new keys and a little reboring. Don't worry! We've been very tactful. Now. Listen.'

He noisily tasted the mouthpiece for a moment, like a little boy with a liquorice sherbet, and then blew. His cheeks filled out enormously, and his eyes closed tightly. At first I thought that he wasn't able to get a sound, but then I was aware of an uncomfortable vibration and the sort of sensation you have when there's a gale in a very old chimney.

'And that's not the lowest note,' he said. 'It goes almost out of range of the human ear and you begin to hear it in the solar plexus. Extremely sensual, in my opinion.'

He was right. When he went on to play a descending scale it was as though a small earthquake was passing beneath me. The tremors travelled down my spine and caressed the perineum. My knees trembled. It jarred the balls of my heels.

'Good Lord,' I exclaimed.

'I got the name wrong, I'm afraid,' said Mr Paul. 'But I looked it up. It's an "Alpenorpheon", invented in 1783 by one Heinrich Muller who was born in Wengen. Rousseau refers to it somewhere. It must be the only serious musical instrument invented by the Swiss, though they're guilty of a fair number of unserious ones, aren't they?'

'How serious is this?' I asked.

'Oh, very,' said Mr Paul. 'The Mozart septet ought really to have one, though the modern editions transpose the part for euphonium. There's an alpenorpheon in the MS score of *Das Rheingold*, and Richard Strauss wanted to use one in *Salome* but was told that one couldn't be found. I dare say there can't be more than a dozen in existence.'

'What can I do with it?'

'You could play the Mozart, of course. But you're right. It's pretty unuseful. I suppose the principle of folding and telescoping instruments to get depth of pitch had to be taken to an extreme at some point, once you'd got the idea with the French horn and the bassoon. This beast really ought to be thirty-five feet long, and as the name suggests, it's meant to move mountains.'

'I have a feeling that's not all it would move,' I said.

He gave me a knowing look.

'There's a story that in its early days the Burgermeister at Wengen was induced to give a soirée at which a consort of no fewer than five of the things played ländler until the small hours. It induced half the guests to take to the Thunersee *au naturel*, there was not a wine-glass left unshattered and the Mayor's wife died of exhaustion on the dancing floor. That season's mothers-to-be called aloud in their cravings not for the usual gherkins or kirschtorte, but for the sound of the Alpenorpheon. And not all those mothers-to-be were married. A scandal in Calvinist Switzerland!

Rousseau is very amusing about it. Eurydice-hysteria, he calls it.'

I gladly wrote out a very stiff cheque for Graveney's, feeling much encouraged by the erotic prospects of the Alpenorpheon. At the earliest opportunity, and after a good deal of tortuous practice, I invited Barbara round for a personal recital. I played till I was white in the face. I played my lungs inside out. I drowned the sounds of the road-works at the Angel. I played Mozart. I played Alberich. I played Salome. I even played Gershwin. It blew my gas fire out. An ashtray juddered across the coffee table and fell to the floor. Half the plastic cases of my CD collection cracked diagonally across. But from Barbara? Not a frisson, not a twitch. So much for the life of passion.

'Is that the thing you bought in Sevenoaks?' was her only response.

I wiped my forehead, and smiled at her with the last tiniest shred of hope that I could muster.

'It is indeed,' I said. 'How would you fancy living there?'

A Transaction

Steffi Grünberg handed over the day's takings to the bank clerk she always dealt with, the dark one with the downcast eyes who always called her 'Fraülein Grünberg' very formally and who counted the notes with an odd little walking motion of his fingers. It almost made her laugh, his way of counting, as though he were imitating little animals to amuse a child. She didn't know why she always went to him rather than any of the others. Perhaps it was because he never made jokes that might embarrass her or asked her to come out with him loudly enough for the other clerks to hear and carelessly enough not to expect her to accept. He was always punctiliously polite, and she knew from the grins that the others threw in her direction that they would have behaved towards her exactly as every other young man of their age behaved. So she instinctively made her way to this one, who was so different.

'Good afternoon, Fraülein Grünberg,' he said, taking the money.

'Good afternoon,' she replied. She could never

remember his name, though she sometimes looked for his little deskplate and thought that she ought really to know it. But it seemed appropriate that he as just one of the bank's minor officers should remain anonymous, while she as the active agent of one of their busiest accounts, the local baker and confectioner, should be addressed by her name. It gave her a sense of importance on her errand. It was perhaps the most significant moment of her day.

'Another fine afternoon, Fraülein Grünberg,' he said, as his fingers began their comic perambulation through the coloured corners of the notes.

'Yes,' she said, noticing the pallor of his skin and the hair thinning above his forehead, and wondering what difference a fine afternoon ever made to him. She couldn't think of him otherwise than as being involved in a mysterious process of abstraction which had begun when customers ordered tarts or truffles. She could understand how the tarts and truffles turned into banknotes, but began to be confused when the banknotes turned into numerals in a machine. However, she was quite content to leave it to others to be responsible for this and further complications of the process.

For the clerk, it was certainly the most significant moment of his day. But whereas the significance for Steffi lay in the drama of the transaction and her role in it, perhaps above all in the trust which had been placed in her, for him the significance lay in an encounter which for once transcended money. Indeed, contrary to the effect produced by the fingers, he quite often miscalculated the amounts. He would have been ready to embezzle for her.

For him the mystery was not abstraction, but embodiment. The mundane biological transactions of the species were in theory perfectly familiar to him. He understood survival, reproduction, mutation. He got the point of lewd jokes whenever he was forced to overhear them. Cinema hoardings emblazoned their myths in his head. His relations married and bore children. His body frequently rebelled.

But what was all this to do with the face of Fräulein Grünberg? With that aquiline nose and sandy eyes, the narrow brow and its expression of quizzical helplessness designed, it would seem, to draw his very heart out of his mouth. His walking fingers trembled as they counted.

He did not know when he had first fallen in love with Fraülein Grünberg. It was hardly an event, more of an intermittent turbulence, like a distant flickering storm on the further shore of the lake. It was beyond his calculation.

Waste

It was quite some time before I discovered that my father had built his whole life upon a paradox.

His watchword was always: 'Don't waste it!' We seemed to be comfortably off, so I imagined that he was forever saying this out of a high moral principle. A piece of string slightly over eight inches long is good for almost nothing at all, but it none the less had to be saved. Small patches of chutney on the side of dinnerplates couldn't be wasted either, but were scraped back into their jars, even though they might be slightly contaminated by food of other texture, flavour or likely longevity. I sometimes wondered if this principle would have to be applied to a painter's oil colours, as I watched our plates like so many palettes being cleaned carefully of their now muddied colours. I would shudder at the thought of finding a green pea in the piccalilli. It seemed to me both gastronomically and aesthetically offensive.

I later discovered that his own family had struggled to maintain the appearance of gentility, so that this inherited principle did have some point after all. Or at least, it had a point when applied to commodities which had some prospective use. Envelopes were carefully slit open, and there was always a roll of gummed paper on the side board. Fair enough. Though I couldn't help feeling, particularly when I first started to apply for jobs, that the outside world might not take our family correspondence very seriously.

The principle also applied, as I soon discovered, to my own person. My essential character, nurtured and cherished within the close family circle, was not for idle disposal upon any common neighbourhood girl. 'Don't waste yourself!' attained a particular poignancy for me during my frustrated adolescent years, as though even the vessel of my manhood had limited contents, like a jar of chutney. I'm sure that my father had no sexual meaning in mind, but I'm afraid that wasting myself inevitably took on for me such a connotation.

I knew, then, why my father never remarried after my mother's death, even though there were opportunities. He liked the idea of choosing a second, younger partner. I knew that from the frequency with which Miss Trotter would come around to play cards, or, later, from finding Meg Brooks slumped knowingly in our kitchen. He liked the idea. He relished the prospect, indeed – and didn't want to waste it! Since he didn't want to waste it, he was going to save it. Like that eight inches of string.

Well, blow that, I thought. It was Oscar Wilde who

said that the only way to get rid of a temptation is to yield to it. That's a paradox, too, isn't it? But it seemed a more fruitful one to me. My father's paradox was utterly sterile. You were just hoarding things up instead of enjoying them.

I left home with, yes, indeed, an ingrained sense of the importance of not wasting life. But I had converted this into the desire to be absorbed by it, to hurl myself into it, to scrape out that chutney jar with my rattling little teaspoon for all it was worth, quite convinced in my excitement that there would be more where it came from.

Well, there isn't always more. Or not more of the same. Never quite the same. It goes when you've used it. Then you've had it. That's my own paradox, I suppose. My own decision not to waste my life, so different from my father's in principle, left me with just as little as he had.

Grooming

I'd just started to shave when I noticed in the mirror that the cat had come up to the bedroom behind me and was licking her paws on the sunny windowsill. Having been fed, and released from the night's confinement, she was now getting herself into shape. She licked between her splayed claws and turned them over like a woman at a manicurist. Then she started licking her chest, which seemed an impossible neck-cricking operation but one which required her laborious attention.

'Hi, puss!' I called out cheerfully, sending a little plosive charge of shaving foam towards the mirror. I felt good. The can of foam was clean and newish so that the half-mask on my face was dense and smooth, and the first pull of the razor left a deep clean path. Was there anything quite so satisfying as that rasping route from ear to chin and the knocking off into piping hot water of the precarious glob of foam? As a boy I always used to find the rolling of snowballs on lawns almost miraculous in the way that with the growing weight of the ball all the snow lifted clear of the grass.

Shaving was as good as that, but better, because it happened on your face and you felt it. I liked almost everything I felt. Knowing it wouldn't always be so made the feeling even better. To be young enough to be perfectly well, but old enough to be grateful for it! To be old enough to make considered choices in life, but young enough to enjoy them to the full!

What a limited life was the cat's! Choice obliterated by habit, mind swamped by sensual indulgence. I could swear that she listened to Mozart, but only for so long as her tail didn't itch. And here she was, sunning herself as usual as though the day itself owed her the attention due a queen.

Up and down over the dampened fur ran the little tongue. It seemed to loosen itself from her mouth just that much further than was credible, as though a whole ribbon of tongue had to be laid out over her body, ready to wrap it up in one narcissistic parcel and then, at that very last minute, drawn back on an invisible spring into her mouth, ready to be rolled out again immediately.

This process would continue by the hour. After half the morning she might feel moderately groomed, ready at least to blink at the sun in acknowledgement of its favours, settling on her straightened paws like a new batsman at the wicket. But after a moment she would again be busy with her tongue, the hind leg vertical like a mast. Would she ever be clean, would she ever be ready? And if so, then for what? What momentous event was she readying herself for? After the whole business she would do nothing but doze and blink in the sun. There was nothing else for her to do all day.

I shook the razor in the water and dabbed it with the towel. I patted my cheeks with cologne. I patted everything. My chest, my pockets. everything in order. The world was out there waiting for me.

I was game for anything.

The Confession

I've got a confession to make. I finally admit defeat. I've tried to be what they want me to be. I know what's expected, and God knows I'd like it all right, but in the end it's just too much.

Who am I confessing to? You might think it ought to be to them, because I've always failed them. But I'm not simply saying I'm sorry. After all, in my way, I've kept up pretty well. I've done what I could, and they must have liked it. They kept on coming back for more. And more. If they kept on at me like that, all of them, more of them, all the time more and more of them, all wanting more, then I couldn't have been altogether hopeless, could I? They loved it.

No, it's to you lot that this is addressed. You, the rivals. The quietly successful. You know what's involved. You take it as it comes. No fuss.

I remember when we were all younger and I was appalled to hear what was required of us. I felt like this then, even before I had any experience. It was always the others who seemed likelier to succeed: the older boys with their appalling information; the nat-

158

urally lewd ones who responded with inventions of their own and an enviable natural enthusiasm; even some of the younger ones with their energy for hints and misunderstood scraps. I don't know which made me more uneasy, the unignorable changes in my own body which bore out these shocking claims and validated the myth, or the eagerness with which you all embraced the faith, the secret knowingness of your predictions, the frequency of your boasts of appetite and performance. For I didn't feel that the former was in any sense a sufficient corroboration of the latter. Strangely not. On the face of it, the strength of these new sensations might suggest that there was some truth in the dirty legends we found ourselves introduced to. But good sense reminded me of the power of the imagination, of our competitiveness in all spheres, our great skill at exaggeration.

Little did I know then! Soon I was to see the truth of it a thousandfold, and our pathetic attempts at ignorant understanding seemed more like an understatement. Well, you are aware of this, too. But whereas you have entered into your inheritance with the maturity and calm appropriate to heroes, I have never really lost the bewildered scepticism of those first years. I can see now that they were lying in wait for us, you, me, all of us equally. But it wasn't so much of a trap as a duty. We were being brain-washed into it with promises of pleasure that were, in final analysis, spurious.

I remember every one. Timmy's mother down the road, setting the tone of the whole thing, even sometimes when Timmy was in the house. Margery Main. Mrs Pelvers, the cleaning lady who liked to pretend that it wasn't happening and would go on cleaning, bending over in the boxroom with a dustpan and brush, keeping time. Helen Jackson. Mary Jackson. Helen and Mary together. Mrs Fellows, requiring utter silence and worship, even though it was she who was on her knees most of the time. Timmy's sister. And these were before my sixteenth birthday, the merest tip of the iceberg.

I won't go on. In any case I couldn't bring myself to mention recent names. These are the truly secret events of life, and since they are unlikely to be corroborated, they had better remain secret. And why does no one admit it, the lie? The lie that it is we who pursue, and they who refuse? Why the unnecessary exaggeration of conquests? Why the pretence of virtue and inviolability?

I've given up wondering what I might desire for myself. Superfluity allows no choice. And I can't agree to maintain the myth any longer. The myth I mean of our crude lumbering expectations, full of rueful overstatement; the myth of their high-mindedness, affectionate condescension and sanctity. All lies. They have the quick eye and ready craw of the dawn thrush. They are as indiscriminate as rain, lavish as flowers.

Come on, admit it! Let's put an end to the charade.

Let's have the truth. Let's have some brotherly soli-
darity here. Let's allow ourselves a little constructive
hatred for once.

The Speculator

Now that I'm relatively secure in my job I can perhaps afford to relax a little. I know I shall never get further promotion but I'm not suddenly going to be made redundant either, and there aren't many who can say that. My job isn't the most exciting in the world, but I understand that it's important. What I observe I record in the Ledger, and what I record is taken away for analysis. I suppose there must be hundreds like me. Perhaps thousands. I call it 'the Ledger', but that's a little joke. It may have been a ledger once, with steel pen and ink and a lonely high stool, but it's all electronic now. Is it financial work then, you ask? To be honest, I've no idea. It seems rather complicated for money, and probably too theoretical. You can usually tell money because there's an interrelationship between the figures. The figures do things to each other. You know – sums.

No, it's something scientific. My figures are more to do with the state of things. There are lots and lots of figures, but they don't seem to do things to each other. I look for patterns in them. I select, identify and isolate these patterns in the ledger. I could do it with my eyes shut.

No I couldn't. Of course that isn't true. But you know what I mean. It more or less does itself. I've got so used to it.

So, now that I can relax a little, I have time to speculate on another matter that has always bothered me. You might say that it's something to do with figures as well, but these aren't figures that come my way. In fact I don't really see any way to get these figures in the first place. Statistically speaking, samples have to be accurate before you can extrapolate from them, and on this particular subject people just aren't likely to tell the truth. In fact it's something that quite a lot of people still don't like to talk about at all, and I assure you that I'm grateful for that. But even if we don't like to hear about it, we can't help speculating. It's natural human curiosity. And it's something we are in fact intensely curious about. So curious that if the figures *did* come my way, to be selected, identified and isolated, ready for analysis, I dare say it would pay my wages. People would pay good money to know about it, to know the answer.

Yes, the answer. It's quite simple. Certainly not a complicated pattern that yields little bits of itself every day and will keep me secure until I retire. Just a single answer to a simple question. Much more like a sum, in fact, where the figures do things to each other and there's a result. *Quod erat demonstrandum*, and a thin red line ruled in the ledger.

I've always wanted to know it. The thing that's done. You can either presume it is happening all the time, or that it never happens at all. But you'll never get at the truth. People lie. People boast. It's something that even doctors aren't allowed to observe. Where would all the information come from? You couldn't trust it.

Sometimes I look at my patterns for an answer, but I'm not equipped to understand them. I've been asked if I find them inspiring, or even beautiful. I don't think that's the point. They are materials towards a truth that I have to leave to someone else. It's someone else's business to make them beautiful.

It's like your life, really, isn't it? You just add day after day to day, and hope it makes sense. There's no answer to it, no thin red line. All the really interesting, really really fascinating things, you've only your own experience to go on.

And nobody's interested in that.

Telephone

It's six o'clock precisely and the telephone's just started to ring. Should I answer it? It might be the polite thing to do. Dickie said I should make myself at home, and said it in the nicest way: 'The key's the key of the whole flat, remember, not just the front door.' Well, I've taken him at his word. I'm lying on the sofa reading his letters and I've made myself a socking great vodka and tonic. This afternoon was a shambles. I've never heard such a set of meaningless presentations in my life. I feel more exhausted than if I'd delivered one myself. I'm going to cut the dinner and give myself a night on the town.

I ought to answer the phone, take a message. It might be something important. But it can't be for me because no one knows I'm here. Except Dickie, and he's expecting me to be at the conference till late tonight. So it's for him, and he won't be back till tomorrow. If I answer it I shall have to explain all that, and say who I am. Boring, boring.

I thought all yuppies had answering machines these days. You could leave it on even when you were at home, so that you could decide whether to talk to the person or not. Perhaps it's become smart not to have one.

It's very persistent. You'd have thought it would have rung off by now, because clearly no one's answering it. They can't know Dickie very well. It's a tiny flat. You can practically see the phone from any part of it. You could make a dive for it if you were very eager, if you were actually waiting for a call, and catch it on the first ring like the father of a kidnap victim. If they're bothering to let it ring like this they must imagine the place is enormous, with a butler walking gravely across miles and miles of parquet. How ridiculous.

They must realise that no one's here. What would be the point of letting it ring so long? I mean, it's been ringing now for an absurdly long time. I should have been counting. I'll start counting now and call it ten rings so far. Eleven. Twelve.

Of course, it's quite wrong to say that they must realise that no one's here. After all, I'm here. But if they did know that I was here they'd surely expect me to have answered it by now. Fifteen. And it's far too late to do so. What would I say? How could I explain why I hadn't answered it earlier? So if they do suspect that I'm here, and there's no real reason why I haven't answered it (and there isn't) why are they letting it ring? Nineteen. Twenty.

And of course it wouldn't *be* me they'd think of lying here and not answering it. It would be Dickie.

So perhaps there is some point to it after all. It could be a code, a cunning way of getting relatively complicated information via British Telecom at no charge. Twenty-five. Suppose it was this Sue, for example, who's sent Dickie this really rather louche postcard with the naked bottoms on it. She could arrange to ring at six o'clock every day and he would know it was her and no one else. He'd let the phone ring for as long as she wanted, and the number of rings would correspond to a message. The more rings, the more exciting the message. Twenty-nine, thirty. It's stopped. It stopped at thirty.

Thirty possible messages! The mind boggles. The first ones could be quite routine and practical. One to seven rings: 'Jim has to be away Monday night (Tuesday night, Wednesday night, etc.).' Eight to fourteen rings: 'Ditto, but I'll come to *you*.' Fifteen rings: 'Cancel previous plans. I'll be in touch.' Sixteen rings: 'Come immediately!' What would thirty rings be? 'I'm just about to take a long soapy bath with that rubber cast you let me make of you and I'm really going to get it right this time.'

Dickie, Dickie, you sly dog. I can't bear it. I'll have to pour myself another vodka.

VII

NEVER SAY NEVER

The Pig-faced Heiress

There was once a merchant, as kindly in spirit as he was successful in business, who scandalised the parish by returning from the East already married and quite wealthy enough to retire. He was suspected of practising the black arts, and those villagers who were in his employment were forever circulating scandalous stories about him. They said that he cured his dairy-woman of a dropsy by sticking needles in her foot, and that he ordered to be delivered from London several finely-ground lenses of a size too large to be used for reading-glasses.

His wife died in childbirth, but not before being safely delivered of a daughter, perfect in every respect except that she had the face of a pig. The merchant had decided to call her Stella, for of all the wonders in the firmament he considered that there was none greater than the miracle of human life.

The parish was of the opinion that this monstrous birth was a divine retribution for the merchant's necromancy and that he would cease it from that moment and take the penitent's path to Canterbury in the spring. He did nothing of the sort, but set about caring for the child himself with the greatest love and attention, though it was said in the village that the midwife had been turned to stone at the sight of her. Only a handful of his oldest and most faithful servants remained in his employment, and out of deference to their feelings he made Stella wear a black velvet mask whenever she left the privacy of her own chamber.

He might have had the child put in a convent. His relatives urged him to do so as a practical investment in intercessionary prayer, an obvious way of attempting to redeem the punishment that had been visited on him. The merchant was indignant at this. He could not believe that so intelligent and sweet-natured a child was a sign of divine displeasure. He offered fifty gold sovereigns per annum to any scholar of the university who would be her tutor, but despite this generous sum was forced to educate her himself.

And this he did to the best of his ability, teaching her the properties of all minerals and herbs, showing her the heavens through his optic glasses and conversing with her in all the languages of his travels. She was an excellent pupil and a devoted daughter, and of course the merchant had long ago learned to ignore the coarse pouches of skin beneath the beady eyes, the slight drool from the misshapen blackened teeth, the glistening snout. For him she possessed the greatest beauty of all, the beauty of intellectual understanding.

And when she obtained her womanhood he did not

see why some intelligent young man should not come to see this too, for her body was sparrow-waisted and comely, and when she played upon the virginals it was as though the angels were telling bedtime stories in heaven.

The merchant was no fool. If for fifty gold sovereigns he could find no tutor for his little Stella he would never for seven times the sum find a husband for her bed. Nothing less than his entire fortune would do as a bait for the marriage, an amount so incalculable that any mere villager's jaw dropped open in the effort to calculate it, and even in the city they were considerably impressed.

The merchant's fortune lured many a suitor, but one sight of his daughter sent them swiftly away. Some who had spent their grandmother's savings on wooing clothes, not realising how unnecessary was a bait to catch bait, fled in terror when they came into her presence.

There was left only Master Cole of Bristol, a phlegmatic young clerk in the wine trade. He had only recently been a student of philosophy at the university and prided himself on his learning. But he was ambitious in the world, and was convinced that a good marriage would be enough to put him into business on his own account. And the merchant's fortune was more than enough.

Master Cole was laughed out of the inns and brothels of Oxenford for having ice in his veins instead of the honest red blood of a lusty youth, and whatever the truth of that it is certain that he cared more for money and philosophy than was usual. The faint odour that accompanied Stella when she came into the room disturbed him not at all. He gave a deep bow, calculating at the back of his mind how many fine freighters fully rigged for the Canaries her dowry would bring him. The number was sufficient to enable him to endure the removal of her mask without a visible sign of surprise, and very soon they were seated together in front of the blazing fire in the merchant's hall, deep in conversation.

Little did poor Stella realise how inadvisable it was to impress Master Cole. She knew well enough that it was not for her beauty that she would be wed, and was aware of her father's offer, but imagined that a future husband would be pleased that she could draw, and converse, and play at chess, and a hundred other social graces. So when they had set up the board she very soon, having the white pieces, moved her King's Bishop to the Queen's Knight's fifth square, having read the *Libro del Arte del Juego del Axedres* of Master Ruy Lopez and in the original Spanish, too, and of course she very quickly won. Being the daughter of her father she could correct Master Cole's geography, and was doubtful of his being able to sell wine to the Turk. No, she did not believe that the number seven was a mystical number on account of the seven planetary spheres through which the soul descends to earth.

174

Perhaps it was for some purely mathematical reason, as for example it is the only real number before ten, without factors? And in any case are there not more than seven planets? And may not our knowledge advance upon that of the ancients? Surely it may. And indeed it was of very little interest how many angelic powers and of what rank were necessary to move these spheres, since the planets themselves moved by the force of their own motion, like tops. Oh, and had they not yet heard of the heliocentric theory at Oxford? How strange. But it was not vital, she supposed, to be very advanced in philosophy to buy and sell hogsheads in Bristol. What view did he have upon the differential calculus?

Her father, who had always encouraged her to think for herself, was listening behind a door and was delighted. How true it was that physical attractiveness was a superficial lure. The intellect was everything.

Indeed it was. And when Master Cole hastened away, making his apologies, the merchant could not understand it at all.

The Tower

It didn't make sense, she objected, being so close to it, being in fact in absolutely the ideal position, not to have walked to the end of the peninsula. She had found the beginning of a path through the maquis, and it was no good his trying to tell her that it wasn't a path. It had donkey droppings. And if its direction seemed improbable then that only confirmed their experience of such paths, didn't it, which in the great heat and steepness and negotiation of rambling thorny shrubs seemed to delight in striking off in a determined obliquity.

'We'll go!' he exclaimed, smiling up at her from his book. It was not the first time he had agreed to it. There could be really no objection to the walk. He was certainly not objecting. But already she was busy with something, as though the matter had been deliberately postponed.

'We'll go,' he repeated, his eyes returning to the page, but she was not particularly intended to hear.

Theirs was the ideal position, certainly. From the terrace of their villa they could see both bays, and behind them, beyond the deserted restaurants and the field with two or three suede cows, the ridge of the little peninsula extended. The dense bushes of fragrant herbs caught the sun at all angles, at all times of the day. There were shadows, and declivities, that indicated promising secrets. The map hinted at a path, even though its outset could not be confirmed, and noted an old tower. She had a great desire to see the tower.

'Won't it be just like the tower at Capo di Mauro?' he had asked. The memory of the circular Genoese battlements, decently restored, with frank tourist access, was fresh enough to lend a note of dispassionate enquiry to his voice. But he knew that it was not a question of accurately judging the tower's distinction. Should they reach it, clearly the fact of reaching it would be enough for by others it could hardly be much visited. It had become, once the question of walking to the end of the peninsula had been raised, 'their' tower. Finding it was the singular aim of the journey, much as the building of it in the first place, all those hundreds of years ago, had its own purpose, whatever that had been exactly.

There had, of course, to be a point to a purpose, even if you weren't sure what it was. Or was an intention satisfying in itself? Since function could so lavishly outlast circumstance (and he searched for a symbol for such outlasting, readily settling on the tower itself) then the whole of history was simply an incomplete exhausting of resources, a wasteful over-provision of purpose, the pathetic thoughtfulness of finally unnecessary intention.

Yes, but there would have been, he supposed, or would have likely to have been, visible pirates, lit cannon, attempted landings, beacons along the coast, that sort of thing. Not now remembered, or not at any rate particularly conveyed by weathered stone. As she walked by him with a plate on which were some peaches, his hand reached out to her intending to cup her hip in brief affection. He was a second too slow, and the arc of his fingers barely grazed the thin coloured stuff of her skirt. He smiled fondly up at her back.

'Let's decide,' he offered.

She thought they had in fact decided. There would not be many days left.

'We'd decided to make our decision today,' he said, putting down his book.

She laughed at that. Deciding to make a decision was nothing at all, was it? It was a paradox, really, because you could hardly decide *not* to make a decision. It would be like . . . oh, what would it be like? She put the plate of peaches down with a small clatter that did not disguise a real irritation. It would be like having decided not to build the tower in one particular place rather than another, when all you had to decide was not to build one at all. In fact, almost everything he said and thought was a paradox these days. His whole life succeeded in very little except cancelling itself out. Why not be positive for once? Why not propose something that was not a paradox? She knew that now they would never get to see the tower.

'Never say never,' he murmured fondly.

It

'You've given it to her, haven't you?' he suddenly said.

She had the pattern out on the carpet and at first barely registered that he had spoken. She rearranged two of the smaller pieces.

'Mmm?' she asked, to establish that she had heard him.

'You've given it to her,' he repeated.

She sat back on her heels, pushing a tired lock of hair away from her face. He didn't look back at her. He seemed to be staring at his knees. She smiled her business-like smile at him, to show that he had her attention, but he didn't elaborate. What on earth could he mean? Had she given who, presumably Angie, what? It almost sounded like an accusation about something that had been lost, was agreed to be stupidly lost and was someone's fault for losing. Or something that Angie shouldn't have, that she ought to know it might be dangerous for Angie to have, like the key to the Volvo. Or her little black dress. As if that would fit Angie now, even if she had wanted

180

to wear it. He'd been funny about Angie recently, bothering to do things with her that he'd never done very much when Angie had really wanted to do them, like oiling her bicycle. How stupid that had been, when he knew that Jennifer's mother nearly always ferried them to school these days and that when Angie went out in the evenings she liked to dress up and go on the bus with her friends. And that made sense, because she didn't want to get hot and bothered, did she? He'd been funny about that, too, and the time Angie had put on lipstick. Why did they need to have an argument about such a thing? She agreed that no one really used it any more, that she herself certainly didn't, but every girl has to experiment. He tried to make some deep anthropological point about symbolic tumescence, and she had to restrain herself there, because she wanted to say that that wasn't the only tumescence that was symbolic, or not so much symbolic as wishful-thinking. But he probably wouldn't have understood. Or would he? Perhaps he'd sensed how ridiculous the conversation was, because he'd said something that was really quite over the top, something about smearing one's erogenous zones with animal grease, and then gone away to get himself a Sol. There was nothing for it, really, but to laugh. But she'd had to do the laughing by herself, hadn't she? And now not only Angie was at fault, though God knows poor Angie didn't do much wrong, but she herself had committed some faux pas out of a

181

reprehensible motherly connivance. Really! Would she be like this if Angie were a young man? She tried to imagine being difficult and restrictive about a son. No, she couldn't do it. If anything she would be more interested in Angie's adolescence if she were male. It would be somehow, well, more exciting. Perhaps that was it. Ah yes, it must be that. He's disturbed by the discovery that his daughter is inevitably becoming a young woman.

She suddenly felt concerned for him, and tender.

But when she got up, grunting and blowing slightly between her teeth at the creaky ache in her back and then making her usual joke of it, holding her hip and waddling over to him exaggeratedly like an old crone, he averted his face from her kiss.

It was then that she realised how far beyond her concern he was, how very lost and how very frightened. She suddenly knew with absolute clarity what the 'it' was, and did not know whether she had it or not, and, indeed, whether she wanted it any more.

The Composer

'I loved it! I loved it!'

Although the words came from behind me and might be thought to be, though emotional and exclamatory, purely impersonal, I knew that they were addressed to me. I could feel them in the nape of my neck. I recognised the voice. It could only belong to one person. Although I had at that moment almost caught the eye of the cloakroom attendant in that polite but vicious crush to reclaim coats which is one of the trials of opera-going, I turned to face its owner.

Sure enough it was Peggy Brattle, looking as she always did as though miraculously constructed out of face-powder. She was standing there in a posture less of the eager greeting that her words might have suggested than of the weary immobility which told me that she was simply queuing like myself. But despite the weariness, evidently in any case the exhaustion of pleasure rather than endurance, she was smiling at me. One of her hands cradled an elbow. The other held up her own cloakroom ticket, in a gesture designed, I thought, as much to indicate that intention to me as

183

to catch my eye. Her smile, then, was one of conspiracy, belonging to a shared aftermath. If I was minded to respond to her remark, so much the better perhaps. If not, it would be put down to that all-demanding quest for overcoats, as though we were refugees and freezing, and not, as we were, flushed with all that human heat and the complicity of hearing for two or three hours a shared music.

That the music had been such as to elicit Peggy Brattle's response I had no reason to deny. The occasion had brought together all the elements usually required – something Italian, comic yet lyrical, the nineteenth century imagining a Middle Ages where romantic love is complicated by, though never threatened by, buffoonery. It had certainly brought a glow to Mrs Brattle's ageing cheeks. It had induced her, what is more, to speak to me across the shoulders of two or three strangers in public tones that announced her pleasure with the confidence, indeed the social recklessness, that she knew for once it deserved. It was as if on behalf of everyone, thrilled, completed and, yes, exhausted as they must be, she could take the risk of pronouncing a common judgement, of setting the seal of approval upon the evening as a whole. And some of our pressing neighbours smiled, with the concurrent sympathy that belonged to the shared experience of the audience that at the moment of dispersal through the foyer we still partly were.

One, however, blatantly did not. At Peggy Brattle's side, immediately to be seen as her companion, though clearly not sharing her enthusiasm, was a smallish sensual girl with long hair. The solemnity of her face, which, though brown, was almost as aggressively unadorned as Mrs Brattle's was pale with make-up, had something almost sullen about it. She was wearing appropriate, even expensive clothes, but she wore them awkwardly. The face, perhaps unwashed, almost consciously sexual, carried an expression of doubt or disbelief. It seemed to be making the attempt to share a celebration, though haunted by the absence of more immediate gratification.

I smiled in response to Mrs Brattle's exclamation, and, taking her in almost instantaneously, I included the young protégé in my smile. Mrs Brattle continued to twinkle, but the protégé ignored me. She was intent on turning instead to her elderly companion to make what may have been meant as a dutiful contribution to the evening's entertainment she had been given, in its own thoughtful way perhaps a payment in kind, though expressed with an intensity of perception that was genuine enough, coming as it did from those sulky downy little lips with all their power to puncture the appalling illusions of art:

'But he's dead!'

Calculations

I had just spoken to Elizabeth when we saw the children. We had rounded the corner of a dark wood where great random sculptures of snow clotted the branches, springing them with their weight and sometimes exploding silently. We had both been private with our thoughts as one very often is in woods, and I said with a burst of enthusiasm which I really felt: 'There'll be an inn at the next village, I'm sure. We can stay there. They'll have wine, and a blazing fire.'

I meant it as a resolution, not a hope. A resolution, a concession, an imaging of the perfect consequence of the occasion regardless of what had gone before. And at that moment, in the brilliance that was waiting for us beyond the gloom of the wood, we saw the children.

They were in the far distance on the hillside, at what must have been the outskirts of the expected village, two children silently waving and shouting on a snowy roof. It was of a pitch and overhang to accommodate the usual weight of snow, and the children seemed to link the mountain with their fields by sliding down it, as though they were sliding forever down the frozen sky.

Their little x and y of gesticulating colour was all there was of movement in the scene before us, except for a wisp or two of smoke from the village beyond. They were like symbols on a page demonstrating a severe truth in scribbles. When one climbed and the other slid it was like a division in algebra, and yet I knew that the spirit inhabiting such movement was pure animal joy. Nearer, we would see the hectic slithering, the mittens clotted with snow, the red cheeks and cartoon balloons of breath. But not yet.

Joy doesn't translate. Five thousand feet up, humanity is a mould, a crust, a stubborn tide-mark. You couldn't possibly imagine any sort of feelings at all. Even at five feet the surface of skin can be an unwitting but efficient disguise.

As I looked across at Elizabeth plodding in her boots, her hands thrust deep in her coat pockets, I felt my face breaking into something extraordinarily like the appearance of a smile, something surely entirely appropriate to my confident promise of warmth and comfort. But she didn't look up. In fact she stumbled slightly. Deliberately, I thought, as though to give herself an excuse to remain unreasonably disagreeable. If so, she had probably sensed my smile and thought it inappropriate after all. The stumble was a function of the smile, both calculated. Joy would have to be postponed.

'Sod off, James,' she said.

The Hypochondriac

Bert Lacey was a cheerful enough fellow, but everyone knew him to be a terrible hypochondriac. At work they wondered how his wife could possibly put up with him, and his wife didn't understand how he could hold down a serious job at all.

'It's my back,' he would say, lighting up illegally well before the tea-break. Wherever he was, he would always be able to find somewhere to sit down. When the big trollies of new loaves had to be moved he always seemed to be sitting down. He didn't make a big song-and-dance about it, but he made sure that you realised that there was a medical reason. He'd be in there like a shot, doing his bit, if only he didn't have this back.

'They don't know anything about backs,' he would say, not without a certain truculent pride at himself providing a tricky example of this difficult part of the anatomy. The sense you got that he not only had to suffer the back itself, but also the contributory ignorance of the whole of the medical profession, was certainly a decisive one. Bert liked to be known as a

189

'case'. It lent a kind of mystery, even a sort of dignity, to the moments when he was forced to succumb to his condition.

I once asked Iris if he had seen any specialists. It had got beyond the point when you could have asked Bert himself just what course his medical treatment had taken. He took it for granted that you had a thorough grounding in the history of his back and associated problems (legs, sometimes; bowels, rather frequently) and would have taken it amiss if you'd started asking too many basic questions.

'Don't ask me,' said Iris, bitterly. 'He says it all began in the army. But he was too young to be in the war, so it couldn't have been anything serious, could it? I mean, he's all right most of the time. Off he goes to the football, like a little boy, but if I need to get him to change a lightbulb, he'll be flat out on the settee before I can ask. Queer, isn't it?'

'Convenient,' I said. But I immediately regretted it, because it seemed disloyal. I couldn't help wondering if he still made love to Iris, or whether he ever had. They had no children.

'Oh, don't you worry,' said Iris, with a great wink. I wondered for a moment if she had read my thoughts. 'I can call his bluff all right. He's a right wool-puller, is old Bert.'

Yes, that was how he was regarded at work, too. So I don't suppose, between 16 Pretoria Terrace and the Vita-Be Bakery, there was a single soul who took poor Bert's back seriously.

All that was to change.

After a strange episode at the bakery, when Bert was yet again at the centre of attention with his unconcealed stoicism, this time not on a bench with a fag, but out in the street, flat on his back on the pavement by the van he'd been loading, he did in fact see a specialist. He had to, because he was taken into hospital.

And there, as it happens, instead of showing him for the charlatan we all thought he was, instead of sending him straight home again to Pretoria Terrace with a familiar prescription, they did some kind of rare operation on him and kept him in for five weeks.

I must say that we all felt bashful at that. We'd been wrong, that was all there was to it, and somehow we had to make up for all the times we'd been hard on him. Iris was just the same, of course. When I went round to see him after he got home, she was almost in tears.

'I'm making him his favourite, lemon meringue tart,' she said. 'Poor lad. You can go up and see him if you like.'

Bert was sitting up in bed, reading the paper. There was a box of chocolates on the bedside table, and he looked quite perky.

'Bit of all right this, isn't it?' he said. And he gave

me a wink that reminded me very much of that wink Iris had once given me.

'There was something wrong with me after all, though none of you believed me. They were quite interested in it up at the hospital. I got written up. It was no wonder that my GP didn't have the first idea about it.'

I said something about being sorry.

'Sorry?' said Bert. 'Don't you be sorry, mate. This is the best thing that could have happened to me. I'm jacking it in at the bakery.'

'Are you paralysed, Bert?' I asked timidly.

'Paralysed?' Bert laughed. 'I'm as fit as a fiddle! There's nothing to stop me keeping wicket for South Molesden, or climbing up Arthur's Knob at weekends, so they said.' He carefully chose a chocolate from the box. 'But I'm blowed if I'm going to waste the opportunity. Nobody believed me when I was in agony. Not even you believed me, and I trust you more than anybody. More than Iris.'

He leaned forward intently from his comfortable mound of pillows.

'No,' he said. 'I'm not going back to work, and I'll not be climbing Arthur's Knob neither. I'm going to make the most of this. I've decided to become a . . . what do you call them? . . . a hypochondriac.'

And he settled back with a smile and a sigh to await his lemon meringue tart.

Theatre

It was so easy to give up Tommy. She always had her husband, after all, and Jack had shown himself to be infinitely forgiving. He seemed to know, with silent tact, when it was time for her to dispose of one of her young men. She would put them out like plants, to see how they would 'do'. Invariably, she thought, they forgot all they had learned and began to droop immediately. Drooping would be followed by withering, and she could not bear to hear of that. Jack had never withered, old as he was (and of course, he was quite a little older than herself, wasn't he?), so it was always a pleasure to come back to him, the dear.

And Tommy was so very young. 'You will get over this,' she wrote, really feeling it to be true. He had an unimaginable life in front of him, much of which it would be quite literally unreasonable to think that she could share. It would be less than generous of her to stand in his way. She would let him go.

The letter was written on their best azure paper, the smaller size, but with their rather satisfyingly brief address embossed upon it with the dignified emphasis

193

of a memorial. The implication behind it, whatever the occasion for writing, was that here evidently was a place, *the* place, from which communications emanated. It was a long-established family centre, almost a shrine. It put recipients of letters at a distance at the same time as issuing a covert invitation to worship. She was conscious, as the fountain pen flowed beneath her fingers in a pale blue script only a shade darker than the paper, that the graciousness of her handwriting perfectly embodied the graciousness of her feelings. She was really quite calm.

Afterwards she put *Der Rosenkavalier* on the record-player, and sat motionless for some time with her handkerchief looped tightly round her thumb, the arm extended, wrist upwards, over the arm of her chair. If Jack were to come in at that moment, she thought, she could turn slowly to face him, and he would understand, without asking her, what had happened. That revelation of a dear familiar face turning from half-profile to full attention, that searching gaze itself receptive to his own, as if she had been waiting there for his entry, would be enough to elicit the knowing squeeze of her shoulder. He would make some neutral remark, perhaps about the dogs, but she would know that he was not only forgiving her but himself feeling for the pain of her withdrawal.

'Well done, duckling,' he would say, as though she had just negotiated a stile.

They would have eaten, and Jack would try to finish

the crossword. She would have been taken back. And she would successfully make the effort not to cry.

The letter was propped on her little bureau. Unstamped, its firmness of will and generosity of spirit seemed provisional. Tommy's name and address in her writing on the envelope spoke only to her, not to him. It was unreal, unformed, inauthentic, yet horribly fascinating, like a great actor picking his nose in the wings before making a tragic entrance. It brought to mind Tommy himself running down his front steps to meet her, wearing that rumpled cricketing shirt he always wore and an expression of goofy enthusiasm for whatever mild afternoon pleasure she had planned for them.

She knew quite clearly just what kind of response her letter really required. It was not a generous letter at all, it was quite acquisitive. It was not a sacrifice but a plea. Not a decision but an ultimatum. The realisation gave her a little trickle of shock inside.

The letter had very nearly even deceived her, for after all, so much of it was true. It was indeed Tommy who would get over it all.

VIII

ABSENCES

Woman and Bat

Timid creature! Anyone would think you had blundered on purpose out of your tree cave just to lurch and flitter above me, pretending not to be noticed. Do you know you are just a shade darker than twilight, and this your one visible half-hour? I must suppose not, and ascribe your flight not to self-esteem but to the last midge-clouds of a warm day. You have come out to dine, and have no interest in my business with a bucket on a hillside, nor with solitude, being a word you seem to embody but couldn't understand.

We are both outside our places of refuge. Really there is nothing to these small daily adventures but the return, is there? I shall clank back to the cottage and take up my studied place in the light which it is now casting from its deep window across the field like a lantern. I shall sit in the dead centre of its four guardian corners of stone, and speak again to that dear face as if I had never left him, not even for a moment of routine escape or duty. The words will be nothing, and yet they will be everything.

Words are made of nothing, and they have a hard

time of it being anything much at all, little performances of tongue and breath and lips. 'The bats are about already.' It sounds like a babble of affection, mother-talk from someone who was never a mother and hardly more of a wife. Only the silence knows how to decode it: 'Speak to me! Speak to me once directly from the heart you have always hidden away!'

There are other evening tasks, and other evening words. Water flows into a basin, like love hoarded against the drought of the soul. More babble. A candle is lit, and the customary words fly about the room, their intended meanings clumsy and trapped, like a frightened wild thing knocking against the beams.

What is it that I really say? What is it that I am really holding back, despite myself? Why do I feel that somehow after all these years love may still not declare itself? Not because it is not welcome, but because for some reason it has to await a signal that it *is* welcome.

Oh, yes he has made many mistakes, and if he doesn't perhaps know of the mistakes that I have made, he can surely guess them. And if he does not guess them, it can't matter now. It is too late for it to matter. We have each waited too long for a signal that is not forthcoming.

The guilt that puts us in this double-bind has already been forgotten. The days open and close upon it like a curtain over dusty webs. And the curtain does open and close, as it has to, and night arrives and departs, concealing and revealing everything, without discrimination: candle-stump, salt-box, knife; the unmoving chair and the sleeves of the hanging coat; the grim larder and the everlasting clock; the sheen of water in the enamel bucket; the shut chest; the photograph.

These twilight moments are the worst, because they give such vain hope that the cycle of darkness and light may be evaded. It is at times like these that I can imagine slipping away out of this life, with you following unquestioningly as if you had never left my side, quite wordless and faithful.

The stream is loud in the still air. Come with me! Come with me now as if every word had been said, and as if there were after all a way for us to go, uncertain yet faultless as the flight of the bat.

Memory

Alice finally found the courage to go through all of Edward's things. She took a gin into their bedroom and sat and stared at the opened wardrobes. She finished the gin and went to get another, returning with the bottle. She decided that it would be better to make a proper start after lunch. She opened the fridge and looked at all the cling-film covered bowls of half-eaten meals and the row of milk bottles, each the memorial of its weekday. Then she went and had a good cry on the sofa.

'Blast him! Blast him!' she wept.

Not having known what she wanted of him while he was alive she was not going to discover it now. What did it all mean? Had she wanted enough? Had she really wanted anything at all, and had she in fact had it? How did one ever know?

What had the years consisted of? All those units and cycles of time, large and small, had passed by in what now seemed a largely undifferentiated stream of experience. Particular memories belonged nowhere, and were harder and harder to get hold of. She had taken it all so much for granted.

She recognised that phrase as the standard rebuke of those, like herself, whose world had been shattered. It meant that whatever had been granted might easily not have been granted, like a wish. Or a bestowal of affection. It had been unlikely, and not to be presumed upon. And now it had completely disappeared.

It was not her love for him that caused her to weep. It was his love for her, which she had lost. In so many ways it must have defined who she was and who she had become, and now she had no means of maintaining that identity at all. Her life was an empty echo of itself. It was like each of his suits, instantly evoking a role, an occasion, even a mood, but empty of the reality. This was true of everything, every toe-cap, every buckle; his glasses; his forty-seven handkerchiefs; the gardening shoes; the box of dwindled ties, de-elasticated pants and belts that had become too small. It was true of the tube containing his citation, which he had never bothered to have framed. It was true of the Chinese dressing-gown in mothballs. It was true of the dusty box of old clothes brushes, leather cases of dress-studs, the hip-flask, the antique Kodak camera. He had removed his vision of her, a true one, without which she was quite at sea; and had left behind all this sacred rubbish, familiar heartwrenching fragments of himself which amounted to nothing at all, a spiritless simulacrum. She would have dearly liked to have come across some secret which might have thrown it all into relief, something to surprise her into truly remembering him as he was when she was getting to know him, something to bring back her love for him.

Her trophy of the afternoon was the camera. She couldn't place it. It wasn't the camera which they had had before 'their' camera. She couldn't, as she held it in both hands, turning it over, remember ever having used it. It had the air, as cameras sometimes do, of knowing secrets. If it could be a premarital camera it could also be an extramarital camera, and in her postmarital limbo Alice handled it as cautiously as if it had been a service revolver. In the little window that counted the exposures there was a figure '6'. There was still a film in it.

She was immediately almost scared. It meant that amongst the husks and trappings there was something real after all, some part of that inner life that first his fatal illness (though she hadn't quite believed it) and then the crematorium (when of course she had to, but still didn't) had removed him from her for ever. The film would contain certain images of things seen by him and never since seen in that way by anyone else, things once chosen by him to be recorded, still locked in their darkness, the black box with springs, clasps, ground glass, shutters, a crude approximation of vision.

Fearful of letting in light, she took the whole thing

to the man in the photographic shop, who said: 'I haven't seen one of these for a very long time.' Then she delivered three big bags of clothes to Oxfam and felt much better. Perhaps it was right that there should be a complete break like this. Supposing she had discovered an intimate diary? It would be as embarrassing as a séance. Didn't she want things to be simply as they had been, and nothing more? Even if her memory of it all was imperfect?

She was so excited, though, when she got the thin packet of photographs home, that she jabbed the earpiece of her reading-glasses into her left eye and made it water. As if she needed to make herself cry, she thought to herself.

The first two were of some church which she didn't recognise, boring perspectives of buttresses. The next was of a girl with long fair hair looking up at the camera, smiling and protesting, obviously not ready to be taken. Her unposed reaction, with eyelids caught sensually half-lowered and the full smile of remonstration frankly intimate, gave Alice a lurch of shock and hostility which she recognised dimly as an emotion she had not felt for a very long time. Her dead Edward being gazed at in adoration by an attractive girl, and the image locked away in their bedroom for God knows how long! An affair, no less, possibly as short-lived as the aborted reel of film, possibly a life-long secret! The jealousy was as precisely and physically identifiable as nausea or hunger, and for a moment simply to feel it, to feel anything after so long, was exhilarating. But in the next moment it collapsed and her old blank loss was remorselessly restored to her.

The girl was herself.

The Children

When the first tourists made their way along the rough track to the lonely end of the valley, asking to see the well, Huw said he had never heard of such a thing. They didn't seem disappointed. They even took some photographs. They behaved as if it were an adventure, and handed coins to each of the tousled and fresh-faced children who frowned at them from behind the farm gate-post.

Huw was surprised that they should give away money like that for nothing at all. His wife said it was because the children were beautiful.

The next couple who came were more demanding. The well had certain powers, they said. Oh yes, said Huw, and what powers might those be? They didn't seem willing to tell him that, but said that they were very eager to find it. The woman looked quite sharply at Huw when she spoke, as though she couldn't believe that he knew nothing about it.

'Are all these children yours?' she asked, pursing her lips at him ponderingly. She had her hands thrust deep into the pocket of a rather old-fashioned flared skirt.

She turned to her moon-faced husband. 'Don't you think that's interesting, darling?'

He was embarrassed.

'I think we should leave this gentleman to his business, Diana,' he said. 'Come on.'

There were many walkers in the valley that summer, most of them couples. Huw tried to avoid them. If they came near the farm he would pretend to be very interested in the underneath of his tractor.

But his wife had other ideas.

'If they've got money to give away,' she said, 'I don't see why we shouldn't encourage them.'

'But it's a mistake,' said Huw. 'It's just a mistake that's got itself into some guide-book or other.'

'So what?' said his wife. And the next time a couple came near, strolling with that sense of if not having exactly arrived, at least being uncertain about where to go on next, she accosted them and took them to the ditch behind the milking shed for fifty pence.

Huw was amazed when she told him.

'You did that?' he exclaimed. 'What did they think? What did they do?'

'They didn't do anything much,' she said. 'I don't think they knew whether to believe it or not.'

'They didn't ask for their money back?'

'Not a bit of it,' she said. 'And they were very nice to the children.'

'Ah,' said Huw, as if that explained everything. 'The children.'

'They looked so unhappy, Huw,' she said. 'I don't think they can have any children of their own.'

'That's a shame,' said Huw. 'Come to think of it, none of these visitors have had children with them, have they? And it's bang in the school holidays.'

'Don't I know it,' his wife laughed. She was baking great rounds of crusty bread for them, spreading the butter on the flat face of the loaf and then cutting off each doorstep with the loaf held firmly against her body until it was all gone, one for each of their grubby, rosy children: for Gwilym, for Mair, for Ivan and for Owain, for Elen and Mererid, for Harri, for Idwal, for Huw number two, and for little Lug.

Eclogue

'Whose are those sheep, do you think?'

'No idea.'

'Are they Owen's?'

'No, I don't think so. We passed the last of his a while back.'

'Such a pitiful bleating, isn't it? Look, there's nothing for them to eat. The field is grazed to mud and they're just standing about complaining.'

'I doubt that sheep can comprehend the idea of complaint.'

'Why are there so many of them? Why are they making such a noise? It's like walking through a concentration camp. I don't like it.'

'There's a simple answer to both these questions. There are a lot of them because the ewes have lambs, and they are noisy because the ewes are calling to the lambs and the lambs to the ewes so they don't get lost.'

'But the whole hillside of them seems lost. It's like a scene from hell. And now they're all coming over to us. Do they think we have something for them? A message from the world of the living?'

'Hay, perhaps.'

'I wish we had some.'

'That would simply gratify your wish to play God. The difference it would make to them is immaterial. You are a sentimentalist.'

'Don't you believe in humane farming?'

'They are going to be eaten. I am simply being practical. Besides, look: they have some hay already.'

'Then why are they so unhappy? Why are they gathered at the gate?'

'I've no idea, but it is almost certainly for a reason we can't guess at, or for no reason at all.'

'I feel for them. Don't you think sometimes that our own lives are like this?'

'Not at all. We may be damned in our animal life and the freedom of the spirit may be an illusion, but we are more interesting than sheep. And we do have control of our own lives.'

'Do we really, do you think? Aren't we just as uncomprehending as they are? Aren't we, too, waiting for relief?'

'Your analogy has always been an argument for extravagant hope. You wish for a beneficent God, bringing hay. What if there is nothing but the facts of the case, meagre rainfall, overcrowding, failing grass?'

'The facts are perceived and suffered. Anything

211

more is beyond prediction. These creatures endure just like us, but there is so much that they do not know.'

'Would you be any happier if they had a talent for debating the matter, as we do? If these wild sounds were more than maternal warning or the filial echo of location, phenomena as crude as gravity? Might a philosophical sheep have a greater chance of contentment? Does truth dispel hunger?'

'Your vision of life is so cruel.'

'Your vision of life is so unreal.'

'I shall never agree with you.'

'It's not necessary that you should. If you did, you might be in danger of turning into a sheep.'

'Thank you. But oh, listen to that one! Like a baleful comic uncle, like a wild silly baritone pretending to drown!'

The Light on the Hill

Whose is the light on the hill, so high that it really wants to be a star? At first I thought it was a star, the first of the evening, the one that twinkles so gravely that it makes the lonely wish for safe harbour.

But it is not a star. It is the light of some madman who thinks that attitude can allow him to forget the follies of mankind. He must be wealthy to build up there. Wealthy and deranged. Imagine the haulage of tile and marble, the grumbling of labourers, the long negotiations about methods of delivery! No road reaches there. Arrival is merely immanence, departure an endless postponement like intimations of death. He hangs there like a hawk with empty talons, like a book on a shelf too high to be read, like an ulcered hermit on his pillar. He might starve in his grandeur, long forgotten by tradesmen.

Only there is this signal, his light that twinkles above us uncurtained, like a knowing beacon but is so tiny that it seems too far for contact. It's a gesture of a kind, but it requires no acknowledgement. It is like a sigh from a creature that would like to be free but knows it cannot be freed.

Here in the valley we have no hopes at all. Our lights are thrown together in the cautious jumble of neighbourliness, village laughter, the shadows on the ceiling; and out on the edge a single dog barking into the night, the sound of planing. It is work and failure that govern our lives. And the drinking that puts an end to both. Our sighs are the resigned glares of the trapped.

Were it not for the fact that no road reaches there I'd be interested in going up one night, just to get a glimpse of his life style, to see what makes him tick. He might not be so bad after all. He might ask me in. I'd be there on his porch with some excuse, and he'd look at me with a kind of relaxed amusement that I'd know wasn't simply snobbishness because it would be promising some fun. There'd be a woman's voice calling out: 'Who is it, Harold? Who's there?' And there would be a note of interest in that bored sulky voice, a curiosity sharpening the sensuousness like pepper and salt on egg yolk. And Harold would smile knowingly at me, turning the watch slightly on his raised wrist as though the elasticated gold segments of the strap had been biting into his skin, as though time itself were a wearisome obligation to him, a man of business after all, to whom a chance visitor was not only a welcome distraction but possibly a long-awaited opportunity. And I would pass over the threshold, glad that I had changed out of my working clothes.

No, I shall never go. That house belongs in another world, which has its own speculations. That is its privilege. After all, though no road reaches there, some other road must come down to it, a road from another valley that has somehow crested the thickly wooded hill. The light seems proud of the fact, as though offering us the triumphant accident of our therefore being able to see it. It has decided to belong somehow to this valley and not the next. We are the view that it has.

Woman in the Wood

I could almost have imagined you were with me in the wood the other day. It felt like virtue and steely resolve not to do so, almost noble, as though such a belief were a trap waiting for me. Avoiding the trap while knowing I'd be there was itself a conscious danger, and perhaps there was a sort of satisfaction in that to compensate for the greater indulgence. I had invented a drama in order to escape tears, a little drama of the not-quite.

I'd left the kitchen on a whim. I was still wearing my apron and my hands left flour marks on the gate like the passage of a ghost. A fret hung in the valley, wreathed in the old oaks like a mockery of the ocean. Beneath it, the wood was damp and still, the trunks twisted as if bewitched. I walked down into it deliberately, as you'd walk into the sea, and it was so close and warm, the air, that it brought a tightness to my chest.

What had called me out there? The oaks were about their business, staggered down the hill, not quite a crowd. There was a bright trail of honeysuckle in one, like stars in hair. I broke some off to take back for the window ledge. Its blossoms were like pale creatures caught on their backs with no way to right themselves, bright exclamations they were, all quite like one another, which is no surprise when you reflect on it. Each blade of grass, each seeded bluebell found its image. The eye was led by resemblances that spoke of the comfort and bounty of kin. Growth itself was a relationship long before it was an adventure. I think I must have been the only solitary creature there.

Perhaps that's why we like going into woods. They draw us in. They contain us. And once inside them, we find out what we are.

I was nothing but myself. I felt unique.

There I was, short of breath, sitting on a mossy boulder. No noise but the stream, a thin pleasant argument of water and stones far below me, hardly visible through the helter-skelter of oaks. This was someone's favourite place, I thought.

I couldn't sit there for ever without expecting an apparition, something which without being thinner than trees might be mistaken for one of them until it barely moved. Or would it have been the other way round? Could my dream perhaps animate a whole troop of wood-spirits?

Sometimes all quiet places seem as populous as graves. I got up to go, feeling conscious of every inch of my stature, almost unwillingly alive to my finger-ends, my boots crushing the grasses. I could think of myself as the very picture of a woman in a wood, one of those where you'd be pleased to guess why she was there or what she was waiting for.

The trap was sprung.

Third Report on the Planet

I now have conclusive evidence that the inhabitants of this planet are not worthy of our continued attention. I am sorry to have to relate this. I have spent some time here, in great danger of being mistaken for one of the smaller, less intelligent of their fellows, and therefore of being eaten. This gross intolerant abuse of power is bad enough, that the stupid and unresisting should be commandeered as a ready source of the carbon needed to produce organic compounds in their bodies by those whose indolence and lack of empathy allow them to do so without a second thought, to do so indeed with relish and resourcefulness. But I have grown used to this and other examples of their cruelty and short-sightedness. That is not my principal complaint.

No, what has shocked me most is their capricious attitude to the reality of their existence and to the recording of unique details of its processes and achievements. In some ways they have no conception at all of the dignity of that task. They do have language, of course, and some rudimentary forms of observation recorded in language which they call 'history' and 'science' and so on, but these are hardly the disciplines we are accustomed to, being for the most part little more than the statement of general principles and broad circumstances. Details, when provided, are almost always of the unusual and the aberrant, and the result is limited, crude and sensational: chronicles of the more notorious arrogators of power, clinical studies of physical defects, bulletins of crime and accidents and so on. The essentials of their individual lives go unremarked.

It would be fair to explain much of this by reference to their undeveloped state. But if it were the case simply that most of their energy is required for the primary task of living, then they might be excused the greater responsibility. But in truth an enormous amount of their attention *is* paid every day to accounts of lives that do not and never have existed! The fortunes of these purely imaginary inhabitants of the planet are followed with a concern that is not often accorded to real ones, not even to those with whom the individuals have a close organic connection. I wrote in my last report about how each one comes out of another one, and how the process is viewed with intense secrecy and obsession. This interest is extended into a lasting concern with either the resulting or originating individual life, certainly not a concern which matches their concern for imaginary individuals. They have far more information about imaginary lives and feel emotions about them that are frequently just as intense and often more intense than those they feel for the ones out of whom they came, or who have come out of them. As for the ones out of whom the ones out of whom the ones out of whom the ones out of whom they came: in almost every case such relatively remote lives are quite unknown. I choose the example at random to show how the phenomenon of 'death' puts at a distance all details of real lives and makes impossible the recovery of them when they have not been recorded and when the necessity of recording them has not been learned. But although such real lives are now unknown, the wholly imaginary ones that they themselves foolishly invented and were obsessed with, are still, even now, objects of interest! The result is that the lives of a hundred years ago are quite obscure, even those of their own forebears, and yet the lives of the false ones (out of whom no real individuals ever came) are well known, even the subject of much speculation and argument.

I find these circumstances quite bizarre. And utterly repugnant.

IX

WAKE ME UP WHEN SOMETHING'S HAPPENING

My Story

Now that I'm slowing up a bit, somebody really ought to come along and take down my story. There's time yet, but they won't have for ever.

What would I tell them? Well now, it's a question of what's important, isn't it? There's a whole load of stuff that they wouldn't want to hear. I roasted the very onions that Cyrus ate on the day that Babylon fell. It was my twin sister who was chosen to be sealed into the Pyramid. She gave me a letter which I was never to open. I broached the Great Wall of China from the north. When my pony collapsed beneath me I lived for forty days in the ice on its raw flesh. I returned with the first gunpowder that the West had ever seen or heard, wrapped in pieces of silk taken from the Porcelain Tower of Nankin. I bought my freedom from the Turks with it and saw them topple the straddling lighthouse giant into the bay at Rhodes, capsizing eighteen galleys. I was the first worshipper at the Temple of Diana at Epheseus and the first Christian to outstare the lions at the Coliseum. With my freedom and noted speed of riding I carried greetings to the seven churches of Asia: in Epheseus I saw a woman branded for consorting with an elkhound; in Smyrna I stayed for the drying of the grape harvest; in Pergamos I ate the raw livers of goats, a delicacy, and contracted a tapeworm; in Thyatira I coaxed it out, sitting for ten days over a chamber of warm milk; in Sardis I gave my last piece of gold for a timber of the Ark, which crumbled to dust in my saddlebag; in Philadelphia I lay with three sisters in one night, daughters of a blind scrivener who beat me at chess; in Laodicea I saw a mountain lion with two heads, stuffed. All these churches are now Muslim, though I had no personal responsibility for that.

Nobody can think of themselves as a character in their own story. Nobody in fact sees their own life *as* a story. You never get outside it to see its shape. If anyone's going to record my story they're going to have to make their own sense of it. Hasn't it been a restless search for something? Or simply a series of distractions and mistakes? One damned thing after another?

Another reason for not believing in your own story is not being able to see how the world can go on without you. But it has to go on without you in order to understand your story and its significance.

Perhaps obscurity would be the better destiny. Stories need resolution, but we have only the desire for achieving a state of things, a stasis, a being, suspended, quite unresolved. We don't want it to stop, whatever the glory.

There is only one story, after all: the story of our bodies telling us that we exist.

A Message for Mr Robinson

There it was again, the pain. Or rather, and much worse this was, the pain was about to come again. It was there in prospect, like the darkening of the sky before rain, like the lit darkness before thunder. He was in unwilling possession of it, as of a rough map of a complicated journey, where getting lost would involve new areas of discomfort and arriving would only consolidate the familiar route he suffered.

Oh damn and blast it!

Would there have to come a point where Mr Robinson noticed? He imagined the heroism of simply collapsing at his machine: it would be what was expected, wouldn't it? The kind of loyalty that the firm eventually rewarded with a reception in the canteen, a humorous speech from the works manager and the presentation of a heavy beribboned parcel by one of the directors? Anything less dramatic seemed craven. What would he say? That he must just stop for a moment? That he would be all right? That no one was to worry? Faint women in department stores said

228

things like that, when chairs were brought, and cups of tea. Nameless ailments, part of life's burden.

He couldn't stop. He had no authority to stop. His pain was not official. It was undiagnosed. He was too frightened of it to want to know what it was.

Mr Robinson was a pink stout young man with a clipped moustache and pale eyelashes like a pig. He was over-promoted, hesitant but dogmatic. He made unpopular decisions but stuck to them. He was in perfect health, his body as clean and fresh as his white coat. It seemed unsullied by any corporeal experience, virgin of pain, innocent of exuded liquids or odours, without sensual volition. Mr Robinson's neat body was the equivalent of his own machine. You couldn't imagine him leaving it untended for a moment.

And now the pain was advancing into its territory like an army with some long-standing political justification. His body was conceding rights that had only ever been tenuously held. The pain was taking his body away from him.

And yet he knew that the pain was in his head. He knew that in extraordinary circumstances it could be ignored, as a soldier, oblivious of a severed hand, could go on to capture a machine-gun emplacement. If it could be put out of one's head, why not into another head?

He stared at the impeccable Mr Robinson over the spinning shafts of his machine, and out of some metaphysical whim to distract himself from the discomfort, he willed the pain to attach itself to Mr Robinson. If he concentrated hard enough, he felt, he could at least make the pain disappear. And if it disappeared, where had it gone to? It felt so much like an invisible presence seeking embodiment, like a restless ghost ready to take advantage of any chink of weakness in bodies. Once called into being, thriving indeed, throbbing in its pleasure at the physical attention of the sufferer like a cat that has jumped on to your lap for warmth, it could not readily disperse. It was mobilised like an army, and had to be maintained.

Transferring it to Mr Robinson was therefore a move of political expediency, to be achieved by some power as formal, attentive and insistent as crisis-diplomacy. Hypnosis, perhaps. He continued to glare at the still apparently unconcerned Mr Robinson, watchful for signs of discomfort. Nothing happened, of course.

He knew that he might just as well have tried transferring the pain to his machine, which couldn't feel its own pain, couldn't feel pain at all, didn't have pain. Would it be preferable to be a machine? Pain was only an extreme function of the sentience that enabled one to experience it. The mind resisted it, out of frustration, as though it were a message it were unwilling to decode. It was no good pretending it was a message for Mr Robinson. It was his, and it was his awareness of it.

He was vaguely aware of the paradox inherent in

this recursive definition, and began to have hopes of it proving a means to outwit pain at last. His mind was now obsessed with his own obsession with it. Surely he had it cornered?

Mr Robinson was writing something on his clipboard. The machines roared.

Resting

I am living with a maniac. Let me roll that one more time so that you get the picture: I am living with a fucking maniac. Truly.

It's never been easy. When we started out together I could never get him to listen to me. These ten little superfluities had more pull for him. Literally. I ask you. It was as if he'd known then that there wasn't much time before they would be pretty well shut away for ever. I had to humour him, and I admit that they had their own kind of poetry, but I should have known then that it would all be hopeless. They were symbols of every distraction that was to come between us, not least that of the eleventh. It's the eleventh little superfluity that should have been permanently shut away, after all; it was rather too often inclined to escape. Well, it does have a justifiable sense of self-importance.

Don't mistake me. I'm not against the Life Force. I voted for it myself! But there is a time and a place for everything, isn't there? It's all this purely imaginary theoretical or prospective perpetuation of the organism that bores me stiff. Most of it is simply speculative. I feel crowded out by dreams and determinations that anyone can see are never going to get anywhere. There's a catch to it that I'd like to tell him about some time. He doesn't see the drift. It's a drift towards extinction. Why else should he want to replicate himself? He isn't going to last for ever. OK, so he's got to make sure of a substitute, someone to take over from him. And how long is that going to take? A few seconds, that's all. Plus a little consequent responsibility. But the business shouldn't take his whole life. It's an obsession with death.

I'm his business!

I sometimes wonder if he remembers that I'm here. There are times, wonderful times, when he hears me. Once he has allowed himself that rare opportunity to give me his attention, he's truly bewitched. I can twist him round my little finger. But it doesn't happen often enough. He may be circulating the planetary fluids (output too brief; input lengthy, but frequently incapacitating) or he may be about to fall into one of his regular self-induced trances. Whatever it is, suddenly he'll notice me. Ah, then we have some times!

Given such general neglect, it's hard to get those inner cameras rolling. The mechanism just doesn't run. And I'm not what I used to be. No, I've no illusions about that. But I'm almost game. Quite reliable in fact, if it's the readiness we're talking about. I practise all day long, insofar as I can. But I do need a bit of direction. Nothing I do on my own has any viable shape. It's just not presentable.

But it's all still there! He's crazy not to pay me any more attention. He could do so much for me. There are roles I could play that he's never heard of. We could create the perfect truth in a tenth of the time that he spends stealing organic molecules from creatures that could be his friends. Am I being pushy? Am I over-ambitious? Tell me if I am, because I don't think so.

I could have been a star.

Ant

Now that I have come to consider our life beneath the eucalyptus tree, I am immediately alarmed. I'm terrified, to be frank, simply by the degree of consciousness involved: consciousness of life, consciousness of knowledge, consciousness of consciousness. Where did it come from, this useless gift? I can't yet conceive of any other life, though the very notion of 'life' must require it. I can't see a way to acquiring knowledge that I don't yet have, but I must have acquired at some point the knowledge that I do have. I can't envisage a return to unconsciousness, but suspect that our life really requires it. It's a life of great directness. Tasks are immediate. They are like other tasks. So much so that existence is merely one series of similar efforts, a kind of trajectory, a chain.

Take the eucalyptus tree itself. The paths include its surfaces, and also detached parts of it. When we return, away from the light, the tree is there as well, the dark parts of it. Light parts and dark parts. The whole living thing and the bits to be carried away.

When the world trembles there are other things to

be carried away. This is the gift of food. And it joins the chain. Whatever can't be managed by two or three. This is our greatest knowledge, the best idea of ourselves that we have. The other, which is nearly as good, is the direction to go in. This direction is also an idea of ourselves, ourselves-in-general.

The chain is a building-chain, where direction eventually leads. It takes many turns, to account for the gift of food, but always in the end goes towards building. Building is many things. It is the carrying of eucalyptus-bits. It is the creation of ourselves, the One Big Thing. It is the direction the chain takes to do all this, and the going and the coming that keeps the chain alive. It is the life of the chain, and the return of dead life. It is above all the new life that begins and ends the travelling chain.

And there is no place for consciousness in it. Ourselves-in-general have no consciousness beyond the shared will of the chain. What would happen if we had? What would happen if I were to share this burden of consciousness as automatically as I would share the burden of the food-gift when it is too heavy to be carried away?

It would be an impossible interruption. The movement of the chain must continue. The paths must be kept open. There would simply be no time to think of all this. As it is, I feel like an exile from the necessary scheme of things, as though what I have discovered is a dreadful secret which ultimately will destroy the principles by which we live. As though it points to this other life of which, as I have said, I can naturally have no conception.

I don't know quite what to do with this consciousness of mine. I hope it won't be noticed. If I can keep it hidden while I go about our business then perhaps nothing very terrible will happen. I don't want to be singled out. I don't want to be made a scapegoat. I shall keep quite calm and work twice as hard. If all goes well I may be able now and again to do some serious thinking.

I shall begin with the most obvious puzzle. I shall begin with the eucalyptus. If there is an answer to it perhaps it will help me to understand the One Big Thing, because I suspect that there is an important connection beween them.

The Origin of Life

How long ago was it that the youngest of the gods slipped away to play at the edge of the world? And was it in anger, or in bored frustration, or in pure idleness? For us, it was surely in the unmeasurable past, almost in the dawn of time. For him, it will seem as if it were only yesterday, the harsh words spoken, the childish escape gratefully accomplished.

He plays now as he has always played, with the rapt concentration that belongs to the rediscovery of the familiar. Over and over again he takes delight in his slight approach and retreat, his stretching and lingering in the maternal shadow, his nuzzlings, his tugging at hems. She is never far away: sometimes turning towards him, protective or encouraging. Her peaceable folds and trailing robes define her as dignified even in her most informal moods. Her profile is all vigilance, her general posture easy and recumbent.

He plays with simple toys that are worn with use, that once were, as are all first toys, parts of her. He turns them over constantly as though there might be some aspect of them that he has never seen, as though placing them in a fresh relationship with each other would answer an old riddle. Perhaps he is telling stories with them, little stories that are models of the mother, tiniest of tiny stories that if a miracle occurred would begin to give an account of themselves on their own without any assistance from him. Over and over they roll, dumb things as yet, that his play animates. He sings to them.

What do the gods make of this? Mostly they take no interest, though the greatest of them stalks by looking down with lofty amusement, and a pretence of directing his fierce gaze elsewhere. This however is the paternal way, and the youngest of the gods is happy to reflect the father's glittering eye with true unconcern. There will be no day in which he will not come, no darkness through which he is not expected. For the darkness no longer holds terrors. The gods are populating the darkness.

And his dumb toys are becoming used to their games. Could it even be that they are learning his song? The song is an extemporisation, borrowed from elsewhere, hardly understood. It is mere god-babble.

But this new thing, part toy, part story, part song, will one day become proud of learning the rules of its game. One day it will surprise itself by making a sound all on its own, a small echo of the god-babble, even less understood.

And having discovered the pleasure of making any

sound, it will then have to learn to make the right sounds.

The Seven Sleepers

Constantine
We stumbled out of the cave, rubbing our eyelids with our knuckles, like toddlers confronting the reassuring light of the grown-up world after a nightmare. You know how they stand there, quietly smiling, uncertain of their welcome at such an irregular hour though anticipating comfort, and the excitement of sharing proscribed activities? Ours had been no nightmare: we had been asleep for 250 years! Hiding from persecution, we woke to a world that had at last accepted our faith. In the valley below the church bells were ringing. We descended gratefully into our inheritance.

Dionysius
Fame is no substitute for self-righteous ignominy. I craved secrecy, the drunken thudding of the blood, the spear-haft on the door, the fist or spit in the face. I want everyone else to be wrong. I wanted to be hated.

John

I suppose it was natural that they should take us for prophets, seven strange men staggering into Ephesus as if in a dream. Though cocooned in our protected youth our beards were the longest that had ever been seen, our robes out of all fashion, no relatives to greet us. We were acclaimed where we no longer belonged. We were in demand, for sermons, for memories, for pieces of our clothes. We had given up everything for our belief and became a living paradigm of the rewards that await those who scorn the world. Our world had, on the contrary, abandoned us. It had retreated into its own completedness, leaving us with an elusive role to play. It is hard being a paradigm.

Maximian

It's wrong to think of our sleep as pure unconsciousness. For me it was rich in dreams of all that I was then attached to, all that, though I did not know it, I was leaving behind. When I woke, my world was lost, the dreams incapable of resolution. I am condemned by my own beliefs for this knee-melting sense of loss, the irreparable disappearance of my family, my friends, and little Erotia with her white grin and her nipples like olives. Now even her great-great-grandchildren are not remembered. Man is dust, and I do not like it.

Malchus

My faith takes fire from my resistance. Nature is irretrievably damaged; all society corrupt. The truth was beautiful because my schoolmaster did not teach it. You cannot measure the distance between the worm and the star. As for this freedom not to be oneself; though it is chanted in Ephesus I defy it. It must be a mistake because now the schoolmasters teach it. I am only a worm, and I will fight to the death to defend my right to assert the fact.

Martinian

I slept for so long that I have forgotten everything. When they fill up my glass and ask the same questions for the hundredth time, I can only smile like an idiot and invent the same replies. I am, thank God, the least celebrated of the seven. I think I would be happy to go back to sleep again.

Serapion

When we woke and discovered our unique history, we quite reasonably expected that we would live for ever. After all, to have dozed for a quarter of a millennium and still be young! It's bound to give you unnatural hopes. We became privileged members of the community. We, who had been smelly outcasts! It turned our heads, and we didn't think that things would ever change. But now we are really and truly old at last. We have become legendary. I'm not sure if anyone actually believes in us any more. We shall all die soon, and the grave is a cave you don't awake from.

Passage

I must have just dropped off. I do hope everyone's enjoying themselves. Not bored? I can't hear many of those tell-tale signs of merriment: whispers, cries broken off, preparation of food. Is anyone there? I thought I heard one of the crew running down the corridor but I must have been dreaming.

I wouldn't have expected us to be there yet. It all takes time, but it's getting warmer, and this morning (or was it yesterday?) I caught a glimpse of a bird through the porthole. Things will be much better when we arrive. I told the steward as much. It's where we all want to be, after all, I said. It's all very well pretending that the getting there's an end in itself. It has to be made enjoyable. I've paid through the nose for it, and a lot of people are working hard to make it a success. Well, I hope you *are* enjoying it. Be my guests!

It's where I was most happy. I know you'll like it. An island, really. Essentially an island, with of course nothing very much to do, but that's the attraction. You give up all responsibility. Rather like a cruise in fact. You give yourself over to others. You're in capable hands. Your loved-ones with you. An idyll. A dream, if you like. I just hope that they're enjoying it too. Not waiting for me to put in an appearance. Are they? Everything's very quiet. Are they waiting for me? They'll have to go on waiting.

Of course, it would be quite hot below deck. I tried telling the Captain as much through this tube, which was silly of me because I knew it wouldn't really be him on the end of it. Perhaps they were fish not birds. Tropical flying fish. The crew are in their tropical ducks after all. I hope there won't be any more fuss. None of that equator ritual. They do terrible things to you and you have to be good humoured and put up with it. I'll leave all that to you lot. You've got the energy for it, giggling out there. You don't need to keep quiet on my account, you know. I'm quite all right. The steward can take this tray away. I haven't touched anything.

Yes, don't worry about me. It's comforting watching the shadows on the glass. I don't want to move my legs any more. I'll see you all eventually. It won't be long now.

Wake me up when something's happening.